Two thousand dollars?

She couldn't afford to donate two thousand dollars!

Callie met Deacon's secretive, self-satisfied smirk, and she immediately knew what had happened. What kind of man would do that for her?

The interest in his eyes sent a pleasant sizzle down her spine. He had a casual, earthy sexuality that reached out to her. She had to remind herself she was...at least possibly...annoyed with him.

A good person would be annoyed with him. Wouldn't they?

She followed him to the door. Her gaze moved involuntarily from his broad shoulders, down the taper of his back, to his attractive rear. A good person wouldn't be watching his rear end either.

She wanted to be a good person.

He took her hand as they walked beneath the arching oak trees. Then he lifted it and held it still against his lips. She felt a wash of helpless desire warm her body and flush her skin. "Can I kiss you?" he whispered. "I want to kiss you."

She didn't even think to refuse. "Yes."

* * *

The Illegitimate Billionaire is part of Harlequin Desire's #1 bestselling series, Billionaires and Babies: Powerful men...wrapped around their babies' little fingers.

Dear Reader,

The Illegitimate Billionaire was very much inspired by my own children and by my nieces and nephews. Writing the story took me back to when they were toddlers, their foibles, their wonder and their delightful take on the world unfolding around them.

Illegitimate and shunned, Deacon Holt is shocked when his billionaire father, Tyrell, makes him the offer of a lifetime—his birthright. In return, Tyrell asks only one thing—that Deacon romance and marry Callie Clarkson and bring Tyrell's grandchildren home.

Deacon refuses. But then he meets Callie, and all bets are off.

Barbara

BARBARA DUNLOP

THE ILLEGITIMATE BILLIONAIRE

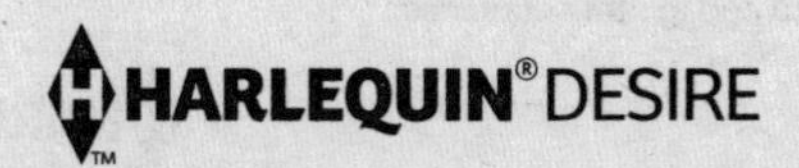

ISBN-13: 978-1-335-97150-0

The Illegitimate Billionaire

This edition published by arrangement with Harlequin Books S.A.

For questions and comments about the quality of this book, please contact us at CustomerService@Harlequin.com.

Printed in U.S.A.

New York Times and *USA TODAY* bestselling author **Barbara Dunlop** has written more than forty novels for Harlequin, including the acclaimed Chicago Sons series for Harlequin Desire. Her sexy, lighthearted stories regularly hit bestseller lists. Barbara is a three-time finalist for the Romance Writers of America's RITA® Award.

Books by Barbara Dunlop

Harlequin Desire

Chicago Sons

Sex, Lies and the CEO
Seduced by the CEO
A Bargain with the Boss
His Stolen Bride

Whiskey Bay Brides

From Temptation to Twins
Twelve Nights of Temptation
His Temptation, Her Secret

Billionaires and Babies

The Illigitimate Billionaire

Visit her Author Profile page at Harlequin.com, or barbaradunlop.com, for more titles.

For Shaina, Jacob, Karl and Heidi

One

In an absurdly masculine room, deep in the halls of Clarkson Castle, Deacon Holt carefully neutralized his expression. He wouldn't give Tyrell Clarkson the satisfaction of seeing anger, envy or any other emotion.

"Drink?" Tyrell asked, making a half turn toward Deacon from the inlayed walnut bar. He held up a cut-crystal decanter that Deacon could only guess held decades-old single malt.

Tyrell was well-known in Hale Harbor, Virginia, for indulging in the finer things.

"No," Deacon answered. He had no idea why he'd been summoned today, after being shunned his entire life, but he was positive this wasn't a social occasion.

Tyrell shrugged and poured two glasses anyway. He cut partway across the library and bent at the waist to set the glasses on opposite sides of a dark wood coffee table.

"In case you change your mind," he said and gestured to one of two brown leather armchairs flanking the table.

Deacon preferred to stand. He wanted to be on alert for whatever was coming.

"Sit," Tyrell said and folded himself into the opposite chair.

Though he was in his late fifties, Tyrell was obviously in good shape. He had a full head of hair, and his wrinkles were few, giving his face character. By any objective measure, he was a good-looking man.

Tyrell was rich. He was clever. He was powerful.

He was also detestable.

"What do you want?" Deacon asked.

The rest of Hale Harbor might jump to Tyrell's commands, but not Deacon.

"A conversation."

"Why?"

Tyrell lifted his glass and turned it in the light that beamed down from the ceiling fixtures. He gazed at the amber liquid. "Glen Klavitt, 1965."

"Am I supposed to be impressed?"

"You're supposed to be curious. When was the last time you tasted fifty-year-old single malt?"

"I forget." Deacon wasn't rising to the bait, even though they both knew he wasn't in a tax bracket that would allow him to casually spend whatever 1965 Glen Klavitt cost. Not that he'd be foolish enough to blow his money on it anyway.

"Sit down, boy."

"I'm not your dog."

One of Tyrell's brows went up.

Deacon expected Tyrell to react with anger. He mentally braced himself for the onslaught, realizing he'd been looking forward to a fight from the moment he walked through the oversize castle doors.

"But you are my son." Tyrell's words, though softly spoken, fell like cannonballs into the cavernous room.

Deacon held still, half expecting eight generations of Clarksons to rise from their graves and rattle the crested shields hanging on the stone walls.

He tried to gauge Tyrell's expression, but it was inscrutable.

"Do you need a kidney?" he asked, voicing the first theory that came into his mind.

Tyrell's mask cracked, and he almost smiled. "I'm in perfect health."

Deacon didn't want to be curious about anything to do with the Clarkson family. He wanted to turn on his heel and walk out the door. Whatever was going on here, he wanted no part of it.

Tyrell had two healthy, living legitimate sons, Aaron and Beau. He didn't need to reach out to Deacon for anything—at least, not for anything that was honorable.

"Will you relax?" Tyrell asked, gesturing to the empty chair with his glass.

"No."

"Stubborn—"

"Like father, like son?" Deacon asked mildly.

Tyrell laughed.

It was the last thing Deacon had expected.

"I don't know why I thought this would be easy," Tyrell said. "Aren't you even a little bit curious?"

"I stopped caring about you a long time ago."

"Yet, here you are."

Deacon knew Tyrell had him there. Despite his anger, despite his hatred, despite the twenty-nine years of resentment, Deacon had come the first time Tyrell called.

Deacon told himself he was here for a confrontation with the man who had impregnated and then abandoned his mother. But the truth was he'd also been curious. He was still curious.

He sat down.

"That's better," Tyrell said.

"What do you want?"

"Do I have to want something?"

"No. But you do."

"You're not stupid. I'll grant you that."

Deacon wasn't sure if Tyrell expected a *thank you* for the backhanded compliment. If he did, he was going to be disappointed.

"Why am I here?" Deacon pressed.

"I assume you know about Frederick."

"I do."

Tyrell's youngest son—and Deacon's half brother, though they'd never been introduced—Frederick had died of pneumonia six months ago. Rumor had it that Frederick's lungs had been seriously damaged as a child, when he'd been thrown from a horse. The fall had also broken his spine and confined him to a wheelchair.

"Did you know he lived in Charleston?" Tyrell asked.

Deacon hadn't known where Frederick lived. He'd only known Frederick had left home after college and never returned. Everyone in Hale Harbor knew Frederick had a falling out with his father and walked out of the Clarkson family's life. Deacon had silently admired Fredrick for doing it.

"Frederick has two sons," Tyrell said. His gaze didn't waver.

Deacon was surprised at that news. He wasn't an expert on spinal cord injuries, but he wouldn't have expected Frederick to father children. He supposed they could have been adopted.

He didn't know what Tyrell anticipated as a response to that particular revelation. But Deacon didn't have anything to say about Frederick's sons.

"The oldest is four, the other eighteen months," Tyrell said.

"Congratulations?" Deacon ventured.

"My only grandchildren, and I've never met them."

"I don't get where this is going." Deacon had sure never met Tyrell's grandsons.

The entire Clarkson family did their best to pretend Deacon didn't exist. Aaron and Beau knew perfectly well who he was, though he'd never been sure about Tyrell's wife, Margo. It was possible Tyrell had been successful in keeping Deacon a secret from her all these years—which begged the question of what Deacon was doing in the castle today. Surely Margo would be curious.

Tyrell took a healthy swallow of the scotch.

Deacon decided to try it. What the heck? It might be the one and only thing his father ever gave him.

He lifted the expensive tumbler to his lips and took an experimental sip. The whiskey was smooth, rich and peaty, not bad, but he'd sampled better. Then again, the company might be tainting the taste.

"I want to see my grandsons," Tyrell said.

"So see them."

"I can't."

"What's stopping you?"

"Frederick's widow."

It took Deacon a beat to comprehend what Tyrell meant. Then he grinned. Poetic justice had visited Tyrell. Deacon took another sip of the whiskey, silently toasting the widow. The scotch tasted better this time, really quite good.

"You find that amusing?" Tyrell's words were terse.

"Someone keeping the powerful Tyrell Clarkson from something he wants? Yes, I find that amusing." Deacon saw no point in shading his feelings. Tyrell couldn't possibly think Deacon gave a damn about Tyrell's happiness.

Tyrell seemed to gather himself, leaning forward, his chin jutting. "Down to brass tacks, then. Let's see if you think *this* is funny. I'll trade you what I want for what you want."

The words unnerved Deacon. At the same time, they put him on alert. "You haven't the first idea of what I want."

"Don't be too sure about that."

"I'm completely sure about that." Deacon had never even had a conversation with his father, never mind confided his hopes and dreams to him.

"I'll acknowledge you as my son," Tyrell said.

It was all Deacon could do not to laugh at the offer. "I could have proved our relationship through DNA years ago."

"I mean, I'll make you an heir."

"Put me in your will?" Deacon wasn't falling for a promise like that—a promise changeable with the stroke of a pen.

"No. Not when I die. Now. I'm offering you twenty-five percent of Hale Harbor Port. You'll be equal partners with me, Aaron and Beau."

Hale Harbor Port was a billion-dollar corporation that had been owned by succeeding generations of the Clarkson family since the 1700s. Deacon tried to wrap his head around the offer. He couldn't.

His entire childhood he'd dreamed of being a part of

the Clarkson family. He'd spun fantasies that Tyrell truly loved Deacon's mother, that he secretly wanted Deacon in his life, that he would one day leave Margo and welcome Deacon and his mother into the castle.

But then Deacon's mother had died when he was barely nineteen, and Tyrell didn't so much as send condolences. Deacon accepted the reality that he meant nothing to Tyrell, and he stopped dreaming.

And now this offer came completely out of the blue. What could possibly be worth twenty-five percent of a billion dollars? Nothing legal, that was for sure.

"You want me to kidnap them?" Deacon asked.

Tyrell shook his head. "That would be too easy. Also temporary, because we'd be sure to get caught."

"But you're not morally opposed to it?" Maybe it should have surprised Deacon that Tyrell would consider committing a capital crime. It didn't.

Tyrell drew in an impatient breath. "Give me credit for a little finesse."

Deacon knew he should walk away from this conversation. "I don't give you credit for anything."

"But you're still listening."

"I'm curious, not tempted."

Tyrell gave a smug smile, polishing off his drink. "Oh, you're tempted all right."

"Spit it out, or I'm leaving." Deacon rose to his feet. He wasn't going to play this game any longer.

"I want you to romance and marry Frederick's widow and bring my grandsons home." Tyrell watched intently for Deacon's reaction.

Deacon didn't have a reaction. He would have bet he hadn't heard right, but Tyrell's words were crystal clear.

"Why?" Deacon tried to fathom the complexity that had to lie behind the request.

Tyrell was reputed to be a master conspirator.

"Why would she marry me?" Deacon voiced his own thought process as he searched for more information. "And what does it gain you? Just offer her money to come home."

"I can't offer her money to come home. I can't even risk contacting her. I'm positive Frederick poisoned her against the family. If I make that play and fail, it's game over."

"You have a whole lot of money to offer."

However Frederick might have disparaged his family, surely most mortal women would be attracted to the family's immense wealth.

"Frederick may have walked away from the company," Tyrell said. "But he didn't walk away from his trust fund. She doesn't need money."

Again, Deacon smiled. "Something you can't buy. Must be frustrating."

"She doesn't know you," Tyrell said.

"Does she know Aaron and Beau?" Deacon still wasn't getting the play here. It had to be galling for Tyrell to approach Deacon for anything.

"Aaron's already married," Tyrell pointed out. "And Beau… I'm not naïve where it comes to my children, Deacon. Beau's nobody's idea of a good husband and father."

Deacon didn't disagree with that statement. Beau had always been the wild one, parties every weekend and a different girlfriend every month. His exploits had been splashed across local gossip columns dozens of times.

"You, on the other hand," Tyrell continued. He gestured Deacon up and down with his empty glass. "I recognize you have a certain sophistication. Women seem to like you. Nice women seem to like you."

Deacon couldn't help but be amazed that Tyrell had paid any attention to him at all.

"You're not publicly connected to the family," Tyrell continued. "You can move in under the radar, romance her, marry her."

"Then blindside her with the news about you?" Deacon had always questioned Tyrell's morality, but this was beyond belief.

Tyrell rolled his eyes. "Ease her into it, boy."

"No." An ownership position in Hale Harbor Port might be Deacon's lifelong dream, but he wasn't going to use Frederick's widow as a pawn.

Tyrell came to his feet. "You have a moral objection?"

"Yes. And you should, too." Deacon peered into Tyrell's eyes, searching for some semblance of a soul. "You do know that, right?"

"Go meet her," Tyrell said.

Deacon started to refuse again, but Tyrell talked right over him. "Just meet her before you decide. If you don't want to do it, don't do it. But don't give up hundreds of millions of dollars without looking at all the angles."

"You're the angles guy, not me."

"You're my son," Tyrell repeated.

Deacon wanted to protest. He might be saddled with Tyrell's DNA, but he wasn't anything like him. He had a moral compass. He got it from his mother.

But he found himself hesitating.

In that second, it was clear he'd inherited some traits from his father. And they couldn't be good traits. Because he was weighing the harm in meeting Frederick's widow. Was there any harm in meeting her before refusing Tyrell's offer?

It was on days like these that Callie Clarkson missed her husband the most. Frederick loved springtime, the scent of roses wafting in the bakery windows, mingling with the cinnamon and strawberries from the kitchen. Today the sun was shining in a soft blue sky, and tourists were streaming into Downright Sweet for a midmorning muffin or warm berry scone.

Their bakery, Downright Sweet, occupied both floors of a red brick house in the historic district of downtown Charleston. The first floor held the kitchen that they'd refurbished when they bought the place five years ago. It also held the front service counter and several tables, both inside and out on the porch. The second floor was a dining room with screened windows all the way around, plus a covered sundeck that overlooked the tree-lined, shade-dappled street.

The lunch crowd was diminishing, and Callie's manager, Hannah Radcliff, breathed an audible sigh of relief.

"My feet are killing me," Hannah said.

She was in her early forties, with rounded curves from a self-described weakness for buttercream. Her voice was soft. Her eyes were mocha brown, and she had a perpetual smile on her very pretty face. Both of Callie's sons, James and Ethan, loved her to death.

"Go take a break," Callie said. "Nancy and I will be fine."

"Rest your feet," Nancy echoed from where she was wiping down the espresso machine. "I'll do the tables."

"I'll take you up on that," Hannah said. "Wait. Hello."

Callie followed the direction of Hannah's gaze to see Mayor Watkins striding past the front window, toward the Downright Sweet entrance.

Nancy gave an amused laugh. She was a college student who had come back to her family in Charleston for the summer. She didn't see the attraction of the Mayor.

Hank Watkins was single, slightly younger than Hannah and equally quick to smile. His dark hair was short at the sides, with a swoop across the top that didn't particularly appeal to Callie. But he was attractive enough, in a distinguished way that was beneficial for a politician.

She'd describe him as burley, with a deep, booming voice. He was the son of one of Charleston's most prominent families. They traced their ancestry all the way back to the Mayflower.

The classic little gold bell jingled as the door opened.

Callie stepped away from the cash register, busying herself with tidying the displays of cupcakes and giving Hannah a clear field.

"Hello, Mr. Mayor," Hannah said.

"You know to call me Hank," the Mayor answered.

"Hank," Hannah said. "What can I get you?" She gestured to the glass case on her left. "A lemon puff pastry? Or coconut buttercream? The cupcakes are popular today."

"What do you recommend?"

"You can't go wrong with the pecan tart."

"Done."

"Whipped cream?" Hannah asked.

"Of course." The Mayor pulled his wallet from his suit jacket pocket. "Callie?" He turned his attention to her.

"Whipped cream is always a nice addition," Callie answered lightly. She kept her attention on the cupcakes, not wanting to intrude.

"I was hoping I could talk with you," Hank said, his tone going more serious.

She went immediately on edge. "Is everything okay?"

Following the unexpected death of her husband six months ago, Callie's optimism had taken a hit. She realized her years with Frederick had made her complacent. She'd forgotten life mostly dished out pain and disappointment. She intended to be braced for it from here on in.

"Nothing too worrisome," he said, handing Hannah a ten-dollar bill. He smiled again as he spoke to her. "Keep the change."

"Thank you, Hank," Hannah said.

He looked at Callie again. "Will you join me?"

"Sure." She untied her hunter green apron and slipped it over her head.

Beneath, she was wearing a white blouse and a pair of pressed khaki slacks. Her hair was up in a casual twist, and her earrings were small diamond studs that Frederick had given her for her birthday last year. She wore them every day. And as she walked around the end of the display case, she twisted her engagement ring and her wedding band round her finger.

She feared Hank was here with bad news about her deck permit.

He had offered to talk to the board personally to advocate for its quick approval. She'd turned down the offer, but now she wondered if that had been a mistake. Maybe she should have let him help.

Frederick had always advised her to keep the local politicians on their side. *You might not love them*, he'd said. *You might not even like them. But it costs nothing to be congenial, and you never know which way the wind will blow.*

If Downright Sweet didn't get the permit to renovate the deck, they couldn't replace the support beams, meaning they'd have to close the deck down while they came up with a new plan. It was May, the beginning of tourist season, and she was counting on running at full capacity by the end of June.

They took an empty table next to the window.

"Is this about the permit?" she asked.

"I'm afraid so."

Callie's heart sank. "It's been denied."

Hank organized his napkin and fork. "Not yet. But Lawrence Dennison is hesitating."

"Why?"

The bakery, along with all of the buildings in the historic district, was subject to stringent renovation conditions. There were bylaws to protect the character of the area. But Downright Sweet's plans had taken that into account. The deck would be larger, but it would be in keeping with the existing architecture.

"Lawrence is Lawrence," Hank said with a shrug. "He remembers the 1950s fondly."

"I can't believe he keeps getting re-elected."

While she spoke, Callie's mind pinged to potential solutions. She could shrink the size of the deck, maybe do only the structural renovations and keep the cosmetics exactly as they were. But it would be a shame to spend all that money and not improve the functionality. And to do a modified application, she'd have to start the process over again, losing time, and she'd definitely have to close the deck for the entire summer season.

"His pet project is the City Beautification Committee," Hank said, a meaningful look in his eyes.

Callie squinted, trying to read his expression. "And?"

"And, if somebody was to...say...join that committee and show a particular interest in city beautification, Lawrence might feel kindly toward that person." Hank took a forkful of the whipped cream and slid it into his mouth.

Callie found the suggestion unsavory. "You want me to bribe Lawrence to get my permit."

Hank gave an amused smile. "Joining a committee is not a bribe."

"It might not be money."

Hank reached out and covered her hand with his.

It was a startlingly familiar gesture. Her first instinct was to pull back. But Frederick's words echoed in her mind. *It costs you nothing to be congenial.*

"Do you have something against city beautification?" Hank asked.

"Of course I don't." Who could have anything against city beautification? "But I'm busy, the boys, the bakery, taking care of the house."

When they'd first moved to Charleston, she and Frederick had bought a roomy, restored antebellum house. It was beautiful, but the upkeep was daunting.

The bakery door opened again, and a tall figure caught Callie's attention. The man glanced around the room, seeming to methodically take in every aspect.

For some reason, he was fleetingly familiar, though she was sure she hadn't met him before. He looked to be a little over six feet, with thick dark hair, blue eyes and a strong chin. His bearing was confident as he took a step forward.

"It wouldn't be much work." Hank's words forced her attention back to their conversation. "I'm the chair of the committee, and I promise not to assign you anything onerous. We meet once a week. There are six members. Depending on the topic, there's usually some public interest, so citizens attend, as well. It's all very civilized and low-key."

Once a week didn't sound like much, but it meant skipping story time with the boys that night, getting a babysitter, doubling up on housework on another evening.

"It's not a bribe," Hank repeated, giving her hand a light squeeze. "It'll demonstrate your commitment to the city, your participation in the community and that you care about the culture and flavor of the historic district."

"I do care about the culture and flavor of the historic district. I live here, and I work here."

"I know." He gave her hand a firmer squeeze. "So join the committee. Join in a little. Make Lawrence happy, improve your city and unblock the permit for your deck."

When he put it that way, other than the babysitting challenge, there seemed little wrong with the plan. It felt opportunistic, but she wouldn't call it unethical.

Hank leaned in and lowered his tone. "With Frederick gone, I'm sure you want Downright Sweet to be as successful as possible."

"I do."

Callie had grown up severely impoverished, never knowing from week to week how her dysfunctional family would afford food, never mind clothes and electricity. Frederick had pulled her out of all that. He'd been a wonderfully sweet man, vital and full of life. The wheelchair had never held him back.

He'd had enough of a nest egg to buy both their house and Downright Sweet here in Charleston. The business had no capital debt, but it was still a struggle to keep operating costs manageable.

A shadow crossed the table, and a deep male voice interrupted. "Excuse me?"

Callie glanced up, startled to see the tall stranger. She looked into his blue eyes and felt a strange pressure build against her chest.

"Are you Callie Clarkson?" he asked. "The bakery owner?"

"Yes." She slipped her hand from beneath Hank's, wondering if the man was a lifestyle reporter or maybe a restaurant critic.

He held out his hand to shake hers.

She took it, and felt a surge of comfort and strength. He was gentle. He didn't squeeze her hand. But his palm was solid, slightly rough, not too warm, not cool, but an identical temperature to her own.

"Deacon Holt," he said.

Hank pulled back his chair and came to his feet, putting on his practiced political smile. "I'm Mayor Watkins. Are you new to Charleston?"

"A tourist," Deacon Holt said, without breaking his eye contact with Callie.

She knew she should look away, but there was something in the depths of his eyes that was oddly comforting.

"Well, welcome," Hank said in a hearty voice. "I hope you've checked out the Visitor Centre on Meeting Street."

"Not yet," Deacon said, slowly moving his attention to Hank.

"They'll have everything you need—hotels, dining, shopping and, of course, the sights."

"I've already found dining," Deacon said.

Callie felt a smile twitch her lips.

"Well, then I hope you have an enjoyable stay."

Deacon didn't seem fazed by Hank's dismissive tone. He looked back to Callie. "What do you recommend?"

"Everything's good."

He grinned at her answer, and the feeling of familiarity increased. "That was diplomatic."

Hank cleared his throat. It was obvious he wanted to get back to their conversation, to hear Callie's decision.

She'd made a decision, but it could wait two minutes for whatever Deacon Holt wanted. On the chance he could offer free publicity, she was going to make him feel more than welcome.

"The sourdough is terrific," she said. "Any sandwich

made with that. If you have a sweet tooth, I'd try a cupcake. The buttercream frosting is to die for."

"Buttercream frosting it is," he said. "Thank you."

"Callie?" Hank prompted as Deacon walked away.

"My answer is yes," she said.

Hank beamed. He really did have an extraordinary smile. He took her hand in both of his. "I'm so pleased."

"When's the next meeting?"

"Thursday. Six thirty."

"I'll be there."

Deacon had been surprised to find Callie in an intimate discussion with Mayor Hank Watkins. Deacon had only been in town a couple of days, but he'd already learned all about the Watkins family. They were the Clarksons of Charleston—all the power, the prestige and the local money.

He'd also been surprised, even more surprised, that Callie was poised, polished and so stunningly beautiful in person. He hadn't expected that of Frederick's wife. Frederick hadn't exactly been suave with the opposite sex.

Deacon had gone to a different high school than Aaron, Beau and Frederick. Deacon had been at PS-752. His three half brothers had gone to Greenland Academy. But there had been enough cross-pollination through sporting events and in social circles, that he'd known the basics of each of them.

He and Beau were the same age. Aaron was a year older, and Frederick was two years younger. Aaron was blond, Beau dark like Deacon and Frederick had ended up with ginger hair and freckles. He was thinner than his brothers and shorter, and always seemed to live in Aaron's intellectual shadow, as well as Beau's athletic one.

Even in the best circumstances, Deacon couldn't see

a woman like Callie falling for a man like Frederick. He supposed it could have been the money. It was often the money. Heck, it was usually the money.

For some reason, Deacon didn't want to think that of Callie. But he'd be a fool if he didn't consider the possibility.

After first meeting her yesterday, he'd waited overnight, waited through the morning, and now he was eating lunch at Downright Sweet for a second time. He was looking for more information, particularly for information on her relationship with Mayor Hank Watkins.

From what Deacon could see, Callie was way out of Hank's league. But Hank obviously thought he had a shot. She must have given him encouragement of some kind.

Fact was, Hank had money just like Frederick. There was a chance Callie's charming personality was an act, hiding a shrewd woman who knew exactly what she wanted.

She was behind the counter now, serving customers and looking as enchanting as yesterday. Her dark blond hair was in a jaunty ponytail. Thick lashes framed her blue-green eyes, and her cheeks were flushed with heat and exertion. Her apparent work ethic didn't dovetail with a gold digger. Then again, most people had contradictions in their personalities. And he hadn't even begun to get to know her.

She'd been right about the sourdough bread. It was beyond delicious. Yesterday he'd gone with black forest ham. Today he was trying sliced turkey and tomato. He hadn't decided on dessert yet. There were too many choices.

His gaze moved from the tarts to the cupcakes to the pastries and cookies. He was tempted by the peanut butter white chocolate. Then again, he could practically taste the strawberry cream tarts. Maybe he'd have two desserts. Maybe he'd have to run ten miles before he went to bed tonight.

He was just about to bite into the second half of his sandwich, when the café door opened. Two young boys rushed inside, followed by a perky teenage girl in a T-shirt, shorts and white runners.

Deacon set down his sandwich and watched the boys with amazement. There was no question that they were Callie's two sons. The four-year-old was a mini version of Aaron, while the eighteen-month-old looked exactly like Beau.

"Mommy, mommy," the younger one called out. He trotted through the maze of tables, while his brother followed at a more measured pace.

Callie smiled at her toddler. "Hello, my little darling."

"We were going to stop for ice cream on Parker Street," the teenage girl said.

She looked to be about sixteen. Her blond hair had a flashy blue streak in it that swooped across her forehead. "But the lineup was nearly an hour long, so they decided to bring all the kids back to the preschool early."

"Did you have fun at the waterpark?" Callie asked.

"Sprinkley," said the compact Beau.

"I went down the big slide." Little Aaron made a long swooping motion with his hand.

"Ethan squirted everything that moved." The teenager ruffled Little Beau's dark head. "He has good aim."

"Squirted James head," Ethan sang out with pride. He turned his thumb and index finger into a gun and pointed at his brother.

Deacon watched the interplay with amazement.

"I was already wet," James said philosophically.

"I'm glad you had fun," Callie said.

"Can we have cookies?" James asked.

"Since you skipped the ice cream, you can each have one."

"I want peanut butter," James said.

"Color candies," Ethan sang out.

"What about you, Pam?" Callie asked the teenager.

"I'm fine."

"We just took some oatmeal monster cookies out of the oven."

Pam laughed. "You talked me into it."

She ushered the boys to a table by the wall.

Deacon rose and crossed to the counter.

"Those are your sons?" he asked Callie.

The question obviously took her by surprise. "Yes, they are."

"They seem terrific."

Her expression stayed guarded. "Thank you."

"Did I hear you say you had warm monster cookies?" Deacon asked.

"Fresh from the oven," she said, putting on a professional smile.

"I'll take one."

"Coming up." She pressed some keys on her cash register.

He held up his credit card. "Your advice was good yesterday."

She looked puzzled.

"You suggested the sourdough bread. You were right."

"I'm glad to hear you enjoyed it." She pointed to the small terminal, and he swiped his credit card over the window.

"I'm back today for more."

"That's what we like to hear."

The machine beeped its acceptance of his payment,

while another staff member set his cookie plate on the counter.

He knew his time was almost up.

"I was wondering," he said to Callie.

Her pretty brows went up in a question.

"Would you join me for coffee?"

The question clearly unnerved her. She touched her wedding ring, and her gaze darted to her sons.

"I don't mean right now," he clarified. "Maybe later?"

Her forehead creased.

"Or tomorrow," he hastily put in, sensing her imminent refusal.

"It's really nice of you to offer," she said.

"I hear a *but* in there."

Was she dating the Mayor? She'd certainly say no to coffee with Deacon if she were dating the Mayor.

"The *but* is that I'm really, really busy."

"I understand," he said, pocketing his card.

Being busy was probably just an excuse. It likely had more to do with Mayor Watkins. But pushing her wasn't going to get Deacon anywhere—better to regroup.

Not that he'd made a decision to romance her. He was still assessing the situation.

He wasn't about to take advantage of an innocent woman. But if she was gaming the rich Mayor now, she might have been gaming Frederick before him. And that changed the equation entirely.

"Maybe another time," he said to her.

"Are you staying long in Charleston?" she asked.

"I haven't decided." He gave her an intimate smile. "It depends on how well I like it."

Her cheeks flushed.

He lifted the plate with his cookie. "Thanks for this."

"Any time."

"I'll hold you to that."

She didn't seem to know how to respond.

He backed off. He'd ask around town. Maybe he'd get lucky and someone would know if Hank Watkins was in a relationship with Callie.

Two

In the small office in the back of the bakery, Callie's gaze rested on the framed photo of Frederick and the boys. She was struck by how much the boys had grown since Frederick passed away. She lifted the picture into better lighting.

It was the last one taken of her sons with their father. It was on their road trip last September. They'd traveled north along the coast, all the way to Virginia Beach.

Frederick had loved driving holidays. She suspected that sitting in a car made him forget about his disability and feel just like everyone else.

James was patient with the long rides, but Ethan was less than enthusiastic about spending so much time in his car seat. Frederick had done his best to entertain Ethan, who had just turned one that trip, while Callie had done the driving. It seemed like such a long time ago.

In November, Frederick had come down with a cold,

just a routine cold that James had picked up in preschool. It settled in Frederick's chest, which was normal for him. He insisted it was nothing to worry about, since both James and then Ethan had run fevers with the bug, coughed a few nights and then recovered.

But in the morning, Frederick's fever had spiked alarmingly. Callie had rushed him to the hospital, where he lost consciousness and was diagnosed with pneumonia. They started antibiotics immediately. But his lungs had been severely bruised in his fall as a young teenager, and the scarring had left them weak.

He never woke up, and she'd said a final *goodbye* to him within hours.

Now she looked at the photo, Ethan grinning on Frederick's lap, James standing with his head on Frederick's shoulder. James still remembered Daddy, but Ethan only knew him from photos and video clips. Both boys had changed so much, grown so strong, learned so much. Frederick would be proud of them both.

"Callie?" Hannah poked her head through the open doorway.

"Is it getting busy out there?" Callie set the picture back down.

It was nearing the lunch hour. Pam had the boys until two today. With Frederick gone, Callie had modified her schedule. Pam was a godsend of a babysitter, and Hannah kept the bakery running like a well-oiled machine when Callie had to be at home.

"The lineup's growing," Hannah said. "The Spring Berry Cheesecake is still really moving."

Callie was happy with the news. They'd created the recipe and introduced the new item just this month. It was gratifying to hear it was a success.

"I'm on my way." Callie rose and followed Hannah through the kitchen to the café.

The lineup was halfway across the seating area. A few tables had just been vacated. Callie moved quickly to clear them and make room for more customers to sit down.

As she freshened the last of three tables, she was surprised to spot Deacon Holt sitting in one of the window booths. It had been a week since he was last in the café, and she'd assumed his vacation had ended and he'd left town.

Since she never expected to see him again, she'd allowed herself to fantasize the past few nights. Her fantasies ranged from hand-holding in the park to kissing under the stars to more, much more. She felt her face warm thinking about it. She knew he couldn't read her mind, but looking at him now felt oddly intimate.

He spotted her. "Hello, Callie."

She shook off her discomfort and went to his table. "Hello, Deacon."

His smile went broad at her use of his name.

"I thought you would have left town by now," she said.

"Still here in Charleston."

She glanced at his sandwich plate. "And back for more sourdough?"

"I couldn't stay away." His tone sounded flirtatious, and she raised her gaze. "I was hoping you'd reconsider my invitation."

She wished she didn't feel the same way. She knew she had to fight it. It would be unseemly to rush out and date this soon after her husband's death.

It wasn't that Frederick had been the love of her life. They were dear friends, companions, parents together.

Frederick had rescued her from hopeless poverty, and she'd given him the family he desired.

"I wish I could," she said honestly.

"Something is stopping you?" His tone was gentle, even concerned.

"A full and busy life." She wasn't about to get into details.

"Someone else?" he asked.

She drew back in surprise. "What?"

"Are you dating someone else?"

"I don't date." She glanced over her shoulder to check the lineup, feeling suddenly guilty for standing and talking while Hannah and the others were so busy.

"Everyone dates," Deacon said.

"No, they don't. Case in point, me." Why was she still here? Why was she indulging herself in something that couldn't happen?

"Maybe not in the formal sense, but the opposite sex is always checking each other out."

"I'm not checking you out," she lied.

There was a gentle amusement in his blue eyes. "Well, I am most definitely checking you out."

"Don't."

"It's not something I can control. But to be clear, I'm only suggesting coffee and conversation."

She gestured to the lineup. "I have to get back to work."

"Okay."

"I can't go out with you. I don't have time." The excuse was perfectly true. Between the bakery and her sons, she had no time for a social life.

"Okay." He gave up easily.

She didn't regret saying no. She wouldn't allow herself to regret it.

She gave him a nod and firmly turned herself around, heading behind the counter.

"What was that?" Hannah asked in an undertone.

"Just a customer." Callie wished she didn't feel overheated. Then again, she was in a bakery, and it was May. It would be odd if she didn't feel overheated.

"He was in last week."

"He was," Callie acknowledged.

Hannah finished ringing up a cheesecake order and handed a customer some change.

Callie took a clean plate from the stack and loaded it up with a slice of Spring Berry Cheesecake, a drizzle of chocolate sauce and a generous dollop of whipped cream. She set it on top of the case, then assembled another identical one.

"What did he say?" Hannah asked.

"Nothing," Callie answered.

"That was an awfully long nothing."

"He asked me to coffee," Callie admitted.

"That's fantastic."

"I said no."

A new customer stepped up. "Two pecan tarts and a dozen peanut butter cookies. Can you make the cookies to go?"

"Cookies to go," Hannah called over her shoulder.

Callie plated the tarts. "Whipped cream?" she asked the man.

"Only on one."

She decorated the tart, while another staff member bagged the cookies.

The staff worked efficiently until the lineup disappeared.

Hannah followed Callie into the back, where cinnamon twists were cooling on racks, and the bakers were rolling out pastry.

"Why would you say no?" Hannah asked her.

Callie knew exactly what Hannah was talking about. "I'm not going to date a tourist. I'm not going to date anyone. I don't have time, and it's only been six months."

"It's been a lot more than six months."

"Nobody knows that." Callie and Frederick had never let on that their marriage was anything other than normal.

Hannah's voice went singsong. "I'm just saying, what's wrong with a little flirting, a little kissing, a little… whatever with a handsome stranger?"

"I'm not answering that."

"Because the answer you wish you could give is opposite to the answer you want to give," Hannah said with authority.

"That didn't even make any sense."

"Your hormones want one thing, but your brain is fighting it."

"I have two sons, a bakery and city beautification to think about."

"Callie, you're a healthy and vibrant young woman who's never—"

"*That* has nothing to do with anything."

Hannah knew Frederick hadn't been able to engage in intercourse. James and Ethan were conceived through in vitro fertilization.

"You're going to have to take the plunge someday."

"Sex is not the only kind of intimacy."

"I get that," Hannah said, backing off.

"It doesn't sound like you get that."

"I'm not trying to push you."

Callie let out a laugh at the absurdity of Hannah's last statement.

"I'm only saying…you know…don't write off a guy like that too quickly. Think about it."

Callie had thought about it. She was still thinking about it. That was her biggest problem. She couldn't seem to stop thinking about it.

Deacon recognized a losing strategy when he was engaged in one. Callie wasn't going to date him. It was probably because of the Mayor, but it could be something else. In any event, if he wanted to get closer to her and find out, he had to change tactics.

He spent another week in town, researching Callie and Hank Watkins. People considered them both pillars of the community. They hung with the same crowd, attended the same functions. People mostly thought the Mayor was a good catch, and a few seemed to have speculated on the two of them as a couple.

When Deacon learned Callie was on the City Beautification Committee, he jumped on the opportunity and showed up at a meeting. He sat in the back, obscured by the shape of the room. But he was close enough to watch her interactions with Hank.

Hank whispered in her ear at one point, and she smiled in return. He touched her arm, and she didn't pull away. He filled her water glass and offered her a pen. She took the pen and drank the water.

Watching her cozy up to the wealthy, powerful, but much older, Hank Watkins renewed Deacon's suspicion she'd married Frederick for his money. It also confirmed that Deacon had competition.

He realized he didn't have the Watkins name and power, and he sure couldn't tell her he was a Clarkson. But he'd achieved a reasonable level of success in life, and he could make himself sound better than he was—richer and more powerful.

But he was going to take a more subtle approach this time, let her come to him. At the end of the meeting, when coffee and cookies were served over friendly chit-chat, he struck up a conversation with a few Charleston citizens. He stood where he was sure he'd be in Callie's line of sight.

"Deacon?" Her tentative voice behind him said the approach had worked.

He turned, feigning surprise. "Callie. It's great to see you again." He cheerfully excused himself from the others.

"Exactly how long is your vacation?" she asked, brow furrowed as they moved a few steps away.

He feigned a guilty expression. "I'm afraid I have a confession to make."

She waited.

He'd rehearsed his lines. "I'm more than just an ordinary tourist."

She looked apprehensive. "Who are you?"

"I'm thinking of relocating to Charleston."

The words seemed to put her off guard. "Why didn't you say so?"

"It's complicated. There were things to check out, arrangements to make. I didn't want people to know I was considering the city."

"Considering it for what?" Now she seemed annoyed and distinctly suspicious.

He realized he was messing this up. "I'm a partner in a national transportation company."

The claim was an exaggeration, but not a huge one. He was a minor partner, and they were more regional than national. But it was true enough to get by.

"We're based out of Virginia," he continued. "But we're looking to expand. We'd need a lot of land, commercial industrial land. If the real estate community knew we were in the market, well, funny things happen to prices when a large corporation expresses an interest."

He stuck as close as he could to the truth. Mobi Transport was always looking to expand. It could as easily expand into Charleston as anywhere else. And local land prices did get jacked up when the real estate community knew a big corporation was in the market.

"You're saying dishonesty was in your best interest."

He wasn't sure how to answer that. "I wouldn't call it dishonesty."

"You're keeping Charleston citizens in the dark about the value of their property."

"I'm keeping the value realistic."

"By lying about your intentions."

"I'm not—"

"That's how market forces work, Deacon. When something is in demand, it becomes more valuable."

He was surprised the conversation had taken this turn.

At the same time, he was curious about her immediate leap to skepticism. Honest people were trusting. Devious people looked for deceit in others.

"I don't want to have to pick another city," he told her. "I like Charleston. If land costs too much here, we'll choose another city where it costs less."

She gave a little shrug, as if the easiest solution in the world was at hand. "Just tell the people that's the case."

"That's one way to approach it."

"It's the honest way to approach it."

"Are you an honesty-is-the-best-policy type?" He watched her reaction.

She hesitated, her expression flinching ever so slightly. "It *is* the best policy."

She hadn't exactly answered, but he didn't press.

"Check out the Mobi Transportation website. See if you think it would be good for Charleston."

The Mobi website was slick and professional. It was designed to encourage sales by making the company look bigger than it was.

"We do long-haul trucking. We have six terminals across the northeast."

Her expression relaxed a little. "That sounds…interesting."

"In the internet age, goods transportation is primed for expansion. There's a whole lot of opportunity in the sector."

Out of the corner of his eye, he could see Hank Watkins making his was toward them.

Deacon gestured to the refreshment table on the other side of the room. "Would you like a coffee? A cookie? They're okay, but not as good as yours."

"Flattery, Deacon?"

"The truth, Callie." He didn't have to exaggerate there. "Your cookies are the best I've ever tasted. How long have you been a baker?"

She made a move toward the refreshment table. "I worked in a café from the time I was fourteen."

He fell into step beside her. "That young?"

"We didn't have much money when I was growing up. I did whatever it took. I lied about my age. I bused tables at first, but then I was promoted to waitress."

He was starting to form a picture of her. She was a survivor. He could relate to that.

"Did you grow up here in Charleston? Decaf?" He reached for the labeled pot.

"Decaf would be best."

He poured them each a cup.

"It was a small town in Tennessee, Grainwall." She flinched almost imperceptibly as she said the town's name.

He kept watch on Hank's progress. "You didn't like it there?"

"Nobody likes it there. My husband, Frederick, and I chose Charleston because it was so beautiful." A look of sadness passed over her face.

"I was sorry to hear about your husband."

Deacon was genuinely sorry about Frederick's death. Frederick had seemed like the nicest of the entire Clarkson clan. He was certainly the most honorable. Neither of his brothers seemed to ever stand up to their father, who—if employees of the company were to be believed—was an ill-tempered, self-centered control freak.

"Thank you," Callie said, her expression pinched. "We miss him. He was a wonderful man."

Deacon silently acknowledged that she played the delicate widow very well.

"I met him at the Fork 'n' Spoon," she said.

"You worked somewhere called the Fork 'n' Spoon?"

"It was aptly named, since we provided both forks and spoons." She gave an engaging smile. "It was mostly burgers and chili—not the best clientele. I don't know how Frederick found it, but he kept coming back."

Deacon wasn't surprised that Frederick kept coming back, and it sure wouldn't have been for the burgers. Callie was enough to draw any man back again and again. Like Hank, who was slowly getting closer.

"He said he liked the chili." Callie held her coffee mug in both hands, but didn't take a drink.

"Was it good?"

She laughed lightly. "I've seen it bring down a man twice Frederick's size. He may have been in a wheelchair, but he had the stomach of an ox."

Deacon decided to let the wheelchair comment slide. "So you moved to Charleston together?"

"That's when we opened the bakery. We had no idea what we were doing. But Frederick had a little bit of money."

A little bit? Deacon couldn't help but be curious about her definition of a lot of money.

"I knew something about the café business," she continued. "And I wanted to work somewhere nice, somewhere pleasant, somewhere that customers were happy. Desserts seemed like a good idea. When Hannah came on board, we managed to make it come together."

Hank was closing in, only one persistent senior citizen holding him back. Deacon glanced at his watch, wondering how he might get Callie outside.

She followed suit and glanced at her watch. "I've got a babysitter waiting."

Perfect.

She set down her cup and started for the door, and he went along.

"You're interested in city beautification?" he asked as they walked.

"I am now."

He held open the door, taking note of Hank's frustrated expression. "Well, that answer has me intrigued."

"I..." She looked flustered.

He couldn't imagine what would fluster her about city beautification. Had she joined the committee to get close to Hank?

"I thought...I should...get engaged and support my community."

Well, that was the worst lie Deacon had ever heard. She was all but begging him to call her on it.

"Will you tell me the real story?" he asked, assuming that's what she expected him to do.

Her face flushed under the community center's porch lights. "It's embarrassing."

"We all do embarrassing things. I promise, I'll understand."

Deacon was ready for her to walk to the parking lot. Instead, she turned the opposite way down the sidewalk. That worked for him.

She took an exaggerated breath, as if she was about to own up to grand larceny. "I joined the committee to butter up Lawrence Dennison."

The unexpected answer threw Deacon. "Isn't Lawrence pushing eighty?"

"Downright Sweet is in the historic district. My deck needs repairs, or I'll have to close it down. I can't do the repairs without the permit. Lawrence is holding up the permit. And the beautification committee is Lawrence's pet project. I'm buttering him up by joining the committee."

Deacon was impressed. By guiltily confessing to such a trivial lie, she looked like the most honest woman in the world.

If Deacon didn't believe she was using the story to manipulate him, it would have been enchanting.

For the next three days, Callie glanced up every time a customer walked through the bakery door. She thought Deacon might stop by Friday. He'd walked her all the way to her door Thursday evening.

He hadn't judged her for joining the committee. He'd understood. He'd even told her his own story about planning a lavish party when a particular state politician was in town, with the aim of getting an introduction to him in order to help Mobi Transportation expand. He couldn't say for sure if it had worked, but he'd definitely put out the effort.

They'd laughed and talked for ten blocks. She would have invited him in, but she had to tuck the boys into bed. She'd found herself hoping he'd kiss her. But he didn't.

Then she'd fully expected him to show up at Downright Sweet and ask her out again. He didn't do that either.

By Monday, she feared he'd left town. Maybe the right land wasn't available. Or maybe taxes were too high. There were a hundred reasons why he could have decided against Charleston.

"Callie?" Hannah came out of the kitchen with a phone in her hand. "It's for you. Lawrence Dennison."

Callie didn't know whether to be optimistic or worried. Was Lawrence calling to thank her for joining the committee, or had he seen right through her ruse?

"Does he sound annoyed?" she asked Hannah.

"Not that I could tell."

"Happy?"

"No. What's going on?"

"Nothing." Callie took the phone. She steeled herself. "Hello?"

"Hello, Callie." Lawrence sounded happy—maybe too happy.

"Hello, Councilman Dennison."

"Please, please, call me Lawrence."

She couldn't help but think the invitation was a good sign, but she didn't want to hope. "All right. Lawrence."

"I'm calling to thank you personally."

She felt a wave of relief. "For joining the committee."

"For the donation."

"The donation?"

Hannah, who was watching, cocked her head in curiosity.

"Two-thousand dollars was very generous of you."

Two-thousand dollars? Had Callie accidentally signed something, or agreed to something? She couldn't afford to donate two-thousand dollars. "I—"

Lawrence didn't seem to hear her. "The beautification committee will definitely put the money to good use."

"Lawrence, I think there's been—"

"And on your building permit, I've reviewed the architectural drawings, and I'm optimistic it can be approved this week."

"Approved?"

She knew she should protest. She hadn't made any donation. And if she had, would it have been a bribe?

Hannah's brown eyes went wide as she whispered. "The permit?"

Callie wanted to nod, but she was afraid to jinx it. Could this really be happening?

"You should hear something by Wednesday. If the office doesn't call, feel free to contact me directly."

Hannah touched her arm, pointing to the bakery door.

Callie turned to see Deacon walk in. He looked tall, handsome and crisply cool in a pair of designer jeans and a dress shirt with the sleeves rolled up and the collar open.

"I…uh…" Her gaze met Deacon's secretive, self-satisfied smirk, and she immediately knew what had happened. "Thank you, Lawrence."

"My pleasure. Goodbye, Callie."

"Goodbye." Without taking her gaze off Deacon, she handed the phone to Hannah. "I have to talk to Deacon."

"Are we getting our building permit?"

"Looks like we are." Callie wasn't sure how to feel about that: happy, guilty, annoyed, grateful?

What kind of man would do that for her?

While she wondered, he came to a stop on the other side of the display case. "Hello, Callie."

"Can we talk?" she asked.

"Sure." He glanced around at the customers. "Can you get away for a few minutes?"

"Yes." She untied her apron and lifted it over her head.

He gave an admiring glance at her white, short-sleeved blouse and fitted black skirt. The interest in his eyes sent a pleasant sizzle down her spine. He had a casual, earthy sexuality that reached out to her.

She had to remind herself she was…at least possibly…annoyed with him.

A good person would be annoyed with him.

Wouldn't they?

Winding her way through the dining tables, she followed him to the door. Her gaze moved involuntarily from his broad shoulders, down the taper of his back, to his attractive rear. He had to be in incredible shape. A good person wouldn't be watching his rear end either.

She wanted to be a good person.

"It's a hot one," he said as they exited to the sidewalk.

"It was you, wasn't it?" she blurted out.

"I don't know," he said easily. "What are we talking about?"

"The *donation*."

It was clear from his expression that he immediately understood. "Ahhh."

"I'm taking that as a yes."

"Yes. It was me. Can I hold your hand?"

"What?" Her brain stumbled on the question.

"Your hand. I'd like to hold your hand while we walk."

"Why are you saying that?"

"Because it's true."

"We're talking about *you* letting *Lawrence* think I made a big donation to the beautification committee."

"We can't do that while I'm holding you hand?"

"Deacon."

"What?" Instead of waiting for an answer, he took her hand as they walked beneath the arching oak trees.

She knew she should pull away, but she didn't seem to have it in her. "Lawrence just called me," she persisted.

"Good." They took a few more steps. "Right?"

It was definitely good holding hands. In fact, it was great holding hands. His was strong. It felt manly. It was a manly hand, and she liked that.

"Callie?"

"Huh?"

"What did Lawrence say?"

"Oh." She put her focus back on track. "He said my permit will be approved on Wednesday."

Deacon squeezed her hand, lifting it to his lips to give it a kiss. "That's fantastic!"

She let his action sink in for a moment.

He'd kissed her.

It was on the hand, sure. But he'd kissed her, and she'd liked it. Her lips tingled as she thought about the kiss. They were jealous of her hand.

She ordered herself to get a grip. She got a grip, tamping down her wayward reaction.

"You bribed him," she said, making sure she sounded disapproving.

"That wasn't a bribe. It was inspiration."

"It was *money*."

"A bribe would be if you called him up and said 'I'll

give you two-thousand dollars if you approve my permit.'"

"I didn't *do that*." Her brained clicked through the implications. "Did I break the law?"

He chuckled. "You're too much." Then he lifted her hand to kiss it again.

He held it still against his lips. He stopped walking, and she stopped too.

He turned to gaze into her eyes. She felt a wash of helpless desire warm her body and flush her skin.

He wrapped his free hand around her upper arm, urging her gently backward into a narrow, cobblestone alley.

"Can I kiss you?" he whispered. "I want to kiss you."

She didn't even think to refuse. "Yes."

Three

Deacon's anticipation of the kiss went way beyond the role he was playing. He truly wanted to kiss Callie senseless. But he forced himself to take it slow.

He brushed the back of his hand over her cheek, marveling at the softness of her creamy skin. "You're beautiful."

Her red lips parted, softening, while her blue-green eyes went opaque. She looked slightly tremulous, compellingly innocent. Even as he questioned her authenticity, he reacted to the sensual image with a rush of passion and an overwhelming surge of possessiveness.

He leaned down and brought his lips to hers.

She tasted like honey. Her lips were tender and malleable. She returned his kiss, and a tidal wave of desire hijacked his senses.

He spread his fingers into her hair, releasing its lavender scent into the summer breeze. He placed his palm on the small of her back, drawing her close, reveling in the touch of her soft, toned body. She molded against him.

Her head tipped to the side, and he deepened the kiss. She welcomed his tongue, answering it with her own. He could feel his arousal build. He was dimly aware they were on the street, barely masked by the stone buildings on either side. He could feel himself stop caring.

But then her palms went to his chest, and she gave the lightest of pushes.

He immediately broke the kiss and backed off. His breathing was deep and ragged, and his head was swirling with a cocktail of hormones and emotions. What on earth had just happened?

"I'm sorry," she said, with a tremble to her tone.

He took another half step back and blew out a breath, struggling to get his bearings. "I'm the one who's sorry. That was my fault."

"It's just…" She glanced to the sidewalk behind him.

"Anybody could have seen us." He finished her thought.

"It's complicated," she said.

He couldn't help but wonder if she meant it was complicated because of her feelings for Mayor Watkins or because of Frederick's recent passing. She still wore her wedding ring.

"I understand," Deacon said. Whether it was Hank or Frederick, Deacon's job right now was the same, behave like a perfect gentleman. "I wasn't trying to rush you or push you. I'd be happy just to take you out for coffee."

A man's voice sounded behind Deacon. "Callie?"

Concern crossed her face.

Deacon turned to see Hank Watkins on the sidewalk behind them.

"Hello, Hank," she said, shifting from behind Deacon,

putting some more space between the two of them. "You remember Deacon Holt?"

Hank's attention shifted to Deacon for a brief second, just long enough to be dismissive.

"I was looking for you at the bakery," Hank said to her.

"Oh?" Guilt was pretty clear in her voice.

Deacon would bet she was either dating Hank, or at least stringing him along.

He decided to test his theory by shifting closer to her. "I don't know if Callie mentioned it, but my company, Mobi Transportation, is looking to open a new terminal in North Carolina."

As Mayor, the prospect should have pleased Hank. But as Callie's boyfriend, it would annoy him.

It annoyed him.

"I see," Hank said, jaw tightening and eyes going hard. "Am I to understand you're considering Charleston?"

"He wanted to keep it quiet," Callie said in a rush, putting the space back between her and Deacon. It sounded suspiciously like she was making an excuse for keeping the information from Hank. "For business purposes," she finished.

"Callie has been very kind in helping me understand the city," Deacon said.

Hank's nostrils flared.

"Did you need to talk about something?" she asked Hank.

Hank refocused his attention on her, and his expression smoothed out. "I spoke with Lawrence this morning. I understand it's good news all around."

"You mean the permit?"

"I mean the donation. Well played, Callie."

"It wasn't—"

"She was just telling me about the positive outcome," Deacon put in.

Hank's gaze hardened on Deacon. "She was, was she?"

"I agree with you," Deacon told Hank, pretending to be oblivious to the undercurrents. "The donation was a good move. The permit should be in place this week, and she can get moving on the renovations."

"*She* doesn't need your support," Hank said.

"I'm standing right here," Callie said.

"Forgive me." His tone dripping with remorse, Hank stepped forward and took her hands.

Deacon wanted to rip her from Hank's hold. He waited for her to break it, but she didn't.

Part of Deacon wanted to repeat his invitation for coffee, nail it down here and now. But the smarter part of him wanted to keep Hank in the dark about his intentions. If Hank knew Deacon was interested in Callie, he'd block him from every angle. Better to make a strategic temporary retreat and let Hank feel overconfident.

"I have to be on a call in a few minutes," Deacon told Callie.

"Sorry to have kept you." She finally withdrew from Hank's hand-hold.

"See you later," Deacon told her in a breezy tone that masked his frustration.

He left them, taking swift, long strides along the sidewalk.

Half a block away, he pulled out his phone. He dialed Tyrell's private number.

"Yes?" came Tyrell's gruff answer.

"I'm in," Deacon said.

There was a silent pause on the line. "You'll romance Callie?"

"Draft the paperwork." Deacon ended the call.

* * *

Callie wasn't going to think of this as a date. It was true that coffee with Deacon had turned into dinner. But that was only a matter of convenience. It was easier for her to get away in the evening. Downright Sweet catered to the breakfast and lunch crowd, closing at six, after patrons picked up takeout on their way home.

She didn't know where she and Deacon were going for dinner, so she'd gone neutral with a sleeveless midnight blue cocktail dress. Its scoop neckline sparkled with a spray of subtle crystals. The waist was fitted, and it flared slightly to mid-thigh.

She'd popped her little diamond studs into her ears, pairing them with a delicate gold diamond chip pendant. Her black, high-heeled sandals were classic and comfortable. Her makeup had turned out a little heavier than usual, and when she caught a glimpse of herself in the mirror, she realized there was a shine of anticipation in her eyes.

She spotted her wedding set in the mirror.

She lifted her hand, spreading her fingers and touching the solitaire diamond.

She was too jazzed tonight for something that wasn't a date.

She closed her eyes. Then she pulled off the rings. Before she could change her mind, she opened her jewelry box and set them on the red velvet. She'd already kissed Deacon once. If she was going to do it again, she had to admit to herself that Frederick was in her past.

She smoothed her dress, taking a last look at herself in the mirror.

Then her phone rang, and she felt a sudden rush of anxiety. Was it Deacon? Had he changed his mind?

She was afraid to look at the number, afraid to see it was him.

"Hello?"

"Callie?" It was Pam.

Callie breathed a sigh of relief. "Are you running late?"

"Yes. I mean, no." Pam's tone was high, her words rushed. "I mean, I'm not running at all."

"Whoa. Slow down. Is everything okay?"

"I fell down the front stairs."

There were voices in the background.

"Are you hurt?" Callie asked. "Who's there with you?"

"I twisted my ankle. My mom's taking me to the hospital for X-rays. It's swelling up fast."

"I'm so sorry." Callie's heart went out to Pam.

Pam was an avid cyclist and tennis player. A broken ankle would be devastating for her.

"I can't babysit tonight," Pam said.

"Don't worry about it. Take care of yourself."

"I'm so sorry."

"It's fine. Get to the doctor. Call me when you know something, okay? And if there's anything I can do."

"Ouch! Mom, I can't bend that way."

Callie cringed in sympathy.

"I better go," Pam said.

"Good luck," Callie called as Pam signed off.

"Mommy, Mommy," James shouted up from the kitchen.

"I'm coming, honey."

The front doorbell rang.

"Ethan squirted his juice box," James cried out.

"Ethan," Callie admonished her youngest son as she trotted down the stairs. "You know better than to squirt."

"Purple," Ethan said with an unrepentant grin.

"Do you want to use a sippy cup instead?"

Ethan's smile disappeared, and he shook his head.

The doorbell rang again.

"Then don't squeeze," she told him firmly.

"Can we have macaroni?" James asked, opening the refrigerator door. "With orange cheese?"

"We'll see," Callie said, swooping the juice box out of Ethan's hand to set it on the counter.

"Juice box!" Ethan cried, reaching up for it.

So much for her date. Or her non-date. Whatever it was, she was sorely disappointed to miss it.

"I have to get the door," she told James.

"Juice box!" Ethan screeched.

"You'll have to wait a minute," she said to Ethan, walking quickly down the hallway to the entry foyer.

She drew open the door to find Deacon on the porch.

"Hi," he said. Then his attention was immediately drawn to Ethan's cries from the kitchen. "Is everything okay?"

"Juice box disaster," she said, pulling the door wide and standing out of the way. "Come on in."

He wore a white dress shirt, a steel blue blazer and dark jeans.

"You look fantastic," he said, closing the door behind him.

She smiled, her heart warming at the compliment. She hated to tell him the night was over before it even got started.

"I'll be right back." She headed for the kitchen to quiet Ethan.

He'd come up with another plan of attack and was pushing a chair toward the counter.

She retrieved the juice box. "No more squirting?" she asked him in a grave voice.

"No squirt," he agreed, abandoning the chair to trot over to her.

"I'm hungry," James said.

"I know." She rubbed her hand over his tousled hair. "Pam can't come tonight."

Ethan took a pause in his drinking. "Pam, Pam."

"Pam hurt her ankle," Callie told them both. "She has to go see a doctor."

"Does she need a bandage?" James asked. "We have horsey bandages."

"Yes, we do," Callie agreed.

The boys were currently big into cartoon bandages. Since they got a lot of cuts and scrapes, it was helpful that they thought of the bandages as a treat.

"The doctor will probably give her a white bandage. It might be a big one."

"Big owie?" Ethan asked.

"I hope not," Callie said.

She was already thinking about tomorrow morning and what she could do about work. With Pam out of commission, she was going to have a problem.

Deacon's voice joined the conversation. "Somebody has a *big owie*?"

Callie turned to see him in the kitchen doorway.

Both boys fell silent and stared at Deacon.

"I didn't mean to abandon you," she told Deacon.

"No problem."

"James, Ethan, this is my friend Deacon Holt."

"Hello," James said.

Ethan stayed silent.

Deacon stepped into the kitchen and crouched on his haunches. "Hello, James. Hi, Ethan. You probably don't remember, but I saw you at Downright Sweet last week. You were having cookies."

"Color candies," Ethan said.

"That's exactly what you had."

"I had peanut butter," James said.

"I had a warm monster cookie," Deacon said.

"Purple juice," Ethan said, holding up his juice box as proof.

"I see that." Deacon's gaze took in the purple streak that ran across the white patterned linoleum.

"Oh, dang," Callie said, remembering the spill. If she didn't get it wiped up, it would stain.

She crossed to the sink and soaked a cloth with hot water.

"I'll get that." Deacon's voice directly behind her made her jump.

"Oh, no you don't." She wasn't about to let him scrub her floor.

"You look way too good to be cleaning floors." He gently but firmly took the cloth from her hand.

"Deacon, don't," she protested.

But he was down on one knee, wiping up the spill.

"Ethan squirted," James said.

"I see that," Deacon answered.

"He got in trouble."

"Trouble," Ethan called out with glee, jumping in place.

"Careful," Callie said, afraid of another stream of purple, afraid it might hit Deacon's white shirt.

"Gone, gone," Ethan said and shook the box.

Callie took it from him, while Deacon rinsed out the cloth.

"It's my babysitter that got hurt," Callie told Deacon. "She's getting an ankle X-ray. I'm sorry, but I'm afraid we'll have to postpone dinner."

Deacon shut off the taps and squeezed the excess water from the cloth. "You're going to have to eat something."

"The boys want me to make them macaroni." It wasn't Callie's favorite, especially when she'd been anticipating music, wine and adult company.

"With orange cheese," James said.

"How do they feel about pizza?" Deacon asked.

Ethan's attention immediately perked up. "Pizza?"

"It has white cheese," Deacon said to James.

"Pineapple," Ethan called out.

"With pepperoni?" James asked.

Callie couldn't believe Deacon was making the offer. Was he actually willing to stay here amongst the grape juice stains with two rambunctious boys and eat take-out pizza?

"What's your favorite topping?" he asked her.

"I don't think you know what you're doing," she said.

"I have ordered pizza a time or two."

"You're volunteering to stay?"

"You're staying."

"Of course I am."

He gave a shrug. "Then that's settled. What's the best pizza place in the neighborhood? And do you want me to run out for some wine?"

On the sofa, Ethan's sleeping head cradled in her lap, Callie sipped a glass of cabernet sauvignon.

"It's the biggest castle in all of England," James said, putting a final colored building brick on the tower he was assembling with Deacon.

"Who lives inside?" Deacon asked, making Callie smile.

"The King," James said. "And the Queen, and five little princes."

"Five? That's a lot of princes."

"They play together in the tower. It has winding stairs, and they have practice swords."

"Are there any princesses in the castle?" Deacon asked.

"Nah. Girls are no fun."

Deacon looked up to catch Callie's eye and give her a lighthearted grin. "I think girls are pretty fun."

"They play with dolls," James said, scooting backward on the living room carpet to survey their creation.

"I suppose that's true. But boys can play with dolls," Deacon said.

"I know they *can* play with dolls. But why would they?"

"They could pretend they were the daddy."

"My daddy had a wheelchair," James said matter-of-factly.

Callie's breath caught for a second. James rarely mentioned Frederick.

"I heard he did," Deacon said with a nod.

"I sat in it once. I like my bike better." James took the remaining few blocks and built a square near the front gate. "That's the statue."

"Guarding the front gate?"

"It's a statue. It can't guard."

"Some statues are built to look fierce and scare off the bad guys," Deacon said. "Like lions."

"Or dragons."

"Or dragons."

"James," Callie said softly, so as not to disturb Ethan. "It's bedtime, honey."

"It's always bedtime," James said on a whine.

"Same time every day," Callie said, although it was

half an hour later than usual. She hadn't wanted to interrupt the castle building.

"It's not fair," James said, screwing his mouth into a mulish frown.

"Why don't we take a picture of the castle," Deacon suggested, producing his phone. "That way, you can always remember it. Do you want to be in the picture?"

Callie couldn't help but admire Deacon's distraction technique.

"I want to be in the picture," James said, coming up on his knees beside the castle.

"Smile," Deacon said as he snapped a few pictures. "I'll send these to your mom, and you can see them in the morning."

"Okay," James said, and then he magically came to his feet.

Grateful, Callie gathered Ethan in her arms.

"Do you need help?" Deacon asked in an undertone.

"He's not too heavy." She stood, wrapping her arms beneath Ethan's bottom, supporting his head with her shoulder. "I'll be right back."

"I'll be here."

She followed James up the stairs, where he tiredly climbed into his pajamas, alternating between jabs with an imaginary sword and wide yawns.

She tucked Ethan in, and then supervised while James brushed his teeth. James was asleep as soon as his head hit the pillow.

Barefoot now, but still wearing her dress, she padded back downstairs to the family room.

Deacon was on the floor, disassembling the castle and packing the blocks into their bins.

"You don't have to do that," she said. "I can clean it up in the morning."

He kept at it. "You're not going to Downright Sweet in the morning?"

"I will if I can find a substitute babysitter."

"Then you don't need to be picking up toys before breakfast."

"Fine. We'll do it now." She lowered herself to the floor to help.

"Am I doing this right?" he asked, indicating the various sizes of bins.

"You're doing it very right. I never thought to ask, but do you have children?" She didn't know why she'd assumed he didn't.

"No."

"Nieces or nephews?"

He hesitated over his answer. "No children in my life."

"Funny."

"Why?"

"Because you're very good at this." She was definitely impressed.

"Good at building toy castles?"

"Good at dealing with children. James was about to make a huge fuss about going to bed, but you distracted him. And you didn't ask if he wanted to demolish the castle. You asked whether or not he wanted to be in the picture. Either answer was a de facto agreement to end the game."

She finished talking and realized he'd stopped putting the building blocks away and was watching her.

"I really hadn't thought it through," he said.

"So it's instinct."

"I don't know what it is, logic and reason, maybe."

She leaned forward, stretching to put a handful of blocks in a bin. "Then I admire your logic and reason."

He didn't respond, and when she looked up at him,

she realized the neckline of her dress had gaped open, giving him an expansive view of her lacy bra.

She knew she should move or cover herself. She didn't.

"Wife?" she asked him.

"Huh?" He didn't wear a ring, but that didn't make it a certainty.

"Are you married?"

He raised his gaze to meet hers. "I wouldn't be looking at you like this if I was married."

"Girlfriend?" she asked, not ready to take anything for granted.

"I *kissed* you."

"That's not a guarantee."

"It is in my case. I wouldn't have kissed you if I had a girlfriend." He eased closer. "Boyfriend?"

"No."

"Potential boyfriend?"

She drew back in confusion. Did he mean himself?

She wasn't sure how to answer.

"I don't really know. I haven't given it much thought."

As she said the words, she recognized they were a lie. She'd given plenty of thought to Deacon. Maybe not as formally as a boyfriend, but definitely in the romantic sense, absolutely in the sexual sense.

"Okay," he said. His gaze returned to her neckline. "You're killing me, Callie."

"You want to kiss me again?" She saw no reason to be coy.

"And how."

She straightened to her knees, and he scooted forward, rising to wrap his arm around her waist, meeting her lips in a deep kiss that sent instant arousal zinging through her. She wobbled for a second, but he held her tight.

On their knees, their thighs were pressed together.

Her breasts were flush against his chest, their bodies pressing intimately.

His kiss deepened. She tipped her head back, giving herself up to the taste and scent and sensation of Deacon.

She wrapped her arms around his neck, and he eased them both to the carpet. The strap of her dress slipped from her shoulder. He kissed the tip. The intimacy of his hot lips on her skin made her soften with escalating desire.

Her body liquefied, melted against him. He slid his hand up her bare thigh, firm, certain and direct. He kissed her neck, then her mouth. He traced her lips with his fingertip. She touched his finger with her tongue, and he groaned, his other hand flexing on her inner thigh.

She knew what was coming.

She wanted it badly.

But she had to be honest. She had to be fair.

"Deacon," she tried, but no sound came out.

"Deacon," she tried again, managing a whisper.

"Hmm?" he asked before kissing her neck.

"You know," she said on a groan as his tongue laved her tender skin.

"I know," he said.

She ordered herself to focus. "You know Frederick."

Deacon interrupted the kiss.

She wouldn't allow herself to stop. "Frederick had a spinal injury."

Deacon drew back, looking somewhat dazed. "Are we really going to talk about your husband right now?"

"No. I mean..." She was afraid of getting this all wrong. "Yes."

"Why?"

She could feel the atmosphere cooling. She had to get on with it. "Because...well...there's something you should know. The boys were conceived through in-vitro fertilization."

Deacon didn't move. He didn't say a word.

"I'm not telling you I'm a virgin," she rushed on. "I mean, not technically. I've had two children. But…the truth is…I've never…" She felt her face heat in embarrassment.

He took his hand from her thigh.

"I'm afraid of doing this all wrong." She took in his stunned expression. "I'm doing this all wrong, aren't I?"

His mouth worked for a moment. "You've never had sex before?"

"I was young when I met Frederick."

"That's a yes? I mean, a no? I mean…"

"I've never had sex before."

He rocked into a sitting position, raking a hand through his hair. "I like you, Callie."

She hated where this was going. She was embarrassed and hurt. "But not enough to have sex with someone so inexperienced."

"*What?* No. *No.*" He emphatically shook his head. "I'm angry with myself. I keep trying to take you on a date. I want to take you on a proper date. I don't want to just—" He gestured around the family room.

She felt instantly better. "Have a quick roll in the toys?" She reached beneath her shoulder blade and extracted a stray building brick, holding it up as her sense of humor returned.

He gave a self-deprecating half smile as he took it from her. "Not my most charming moment."

"It felt pretty good to me."

He reached out to smooth her hair from her face. "Let me take you to dinner."

"I tried to let you. Events conspired against us."

He chuckled low. “They did. Let’s try again.” He put her strap back onto her shoulder and smoothed her hem into place.

“Is our date over?” she asked, telling herself not to be disappointed.

He was being noble. She should appreciate that.

“Tonight might be over, but our date hasn’t even started.”

Four

Deacon wanted to get it right this time. He couldn't remember ever having so much trouble getting a woman on a date.

He wasn't big on labels and designers, but he spent an afternoon in Columbia decking himself out with the subtle symbols of wealth and privilege. He bought a ridiculously expensive watch, a beautifully cut suit, a pair of diamond cufflinks and shoes that cost as much as a new refrigerator.

He hated to admit they were comfortable.

Callie hadn't denied having boyfriend prospects, and Deacon could only assume she'd meant Hank. It seemed she was carrying on with an upwardly mobile life. Frederick had lifted her from poverty, and now she was moving to the next rung, power and societal position.

Deacon could understand that. He might not admire her methods, but he had no quarrel with her objectives.

And if wealth was what she wanted, wealth is what Deacon would project.

It was dead easy to guess at Hank's interest. Callie was absolutely a prize. She would be good for his political career—a beautiful young widow, a business owner in the community, the mother of two little boys. The four of them would look spectacular on the Mayor's Christmas card.

She'd suggested they meet at the restaurant, so he'd arrived at the Skyblue Bistro a few minutes early. When he saw her coming across the walkway, her motivations flew from his mind.

Her hair was loose, billowing around her face in the fresh breeze. She wore a burgundy cocktail dress, slim fitting, with a halter neckline. It molded over her breasts and hugged her trim waist, highlighting a shape that made men turn their heads. The skirt showed off several inches of toned thigh, while her shapely calves ended in strappy sandals that decorated her ankles and polished toes.

He walked forward to meet her. As she drew closer, her turquoise eyes sparkled under the hundreds of little lights in the trees around them.

"Hi." He held out his crooked arm, anticipating her touch.

She took it. "Hi, yourself."

"You look stunning." He covered her hand with his, impatient for skin-on-skin contact.

She cocked her head and took in his outfit. "As do you."

"The most attractive thing about me is walking beside me."

She grinned, and he felt her essence rush through him.

"How was your day?" He told himself to get a grip.

"Hectic. One of the ovens broke down, and we had repairmen there for three hours."

"I'm sorry to hear that."

Before she could respond, they came to the hostess podium.

The woman gave them a professional smile. "Good evening."

"A reservation for Holt," Deacon said.

"Would you like to sit inside or on the patio?" she asked.

He looked to Callie.

"It would be nice to overlook the river," she said.

"The wind's coming up," the hostess said, as she stacked two leather-bound menus. "But I can put you behind a plexiglass divider."

"Does that work for you?" he asked Callie.

"It sounds perfect."

"We'll take it," he said.

The hostess led them to a small table at the edge of the patio. The wind was gusty, but it was calmer behind the divider, and they had a great view of the lights across the river. Clouds were gathering to block out the stars, but the roof above them would keep away any rain.

"Did they fix the oven?" Deacon asked, picking up the conversation thread, as Callie got settled into the padded chair.

"Not yet. They had to order a component from Philadelphia."

"How long will that take?"

"About three days. We bought that oven used when we remodeled the kitchen. I'm not sure it was good value."

"You bought a used oven?" Deacon was confused by that decision.

She gave an absent nod as she opened her menu. "I'm sorry we did. It's been a money pit ever since."

"Why would you buy a used oven?"

"It was reconditioned. We also bought two that were new, smaller ones. To get *that* size, in a decent brand, would have cost the earth. You probably haven't eaten here yet. The steaks are amazing, but the fish is their feature. It's always market fresh."

"Frederick bought a *used* bakery oven?"

She looked up, her brow wrinkling. "Why is that so surprising? Back then, we had to economize where we could."

"Why?"

It took her a moment to answer. "The usual reasons."

Deacon gave himself a shake, realizing he was grilling her. "I'm sorry. I don't know where I got the impression Frederick had a lot of money."

"He had some. Way more than I ever imagined having, that's for sure."

Deacon wanted to probe for more information, but he didn't dare.

"Shall I order a bottle of wine?" he asked instead.

"I'd drink a glass or two."

"Red or white?"

"What are you ordering for dinner?" she asked.

"You say they're good with fish?"

"It's hard to go wrong with the catch of the day."

He flipped to the white wine page and turned the list toward her. "What looks good to you?"

"I don't know anything about wines."

"Frederick did the wine ordering?" Deacon guessed.

"We weren't that big into them. We pretty much went with what was on sale."

That didn't sound even remotely right to Deacon. She

was obviously downplaying her lifestyle. The question was why?

The waiter appeared, along with an assistant who filled their water glasses.

"My name is Henri, and I'll be serving you tonight, along with Alex and Patricia," he said, gesturing to the woman beside him. "Can I start you off with a cocktail or an appetizer?"

Deacon looked to Callie. "A cocktail?"

"Wine is fine for me."

Deacon looked down at the wine list and pointed to the most expensive white on the page.

"The Minz Valley Grand Cru," Henri confirmed. "We receive excellent feedback on that one."

He placed their napkins in their laps before withdrawing.

The wind picked up, flickering the flame in the glass hurricane lamp and billowing the tablecloth.

Callie brushed her hair from her face, but it blew right back again. "Will it totally ruin my look if I pull my hair back?"

"Nothing could ruin your look."

"Good answer."

She fumbled with her purse, producing a clip that she set on the table. Then she worked against the wind to pull her hair to the back of her head.

"Do you need some help?" he asked.

"Can you hand it to me?" She nodded to the tortoise shell clip.

He handed it over, and she snapped it into her hair.

"That's better," she said.

"We can go inside," he offered.

"No, I like the breeze. I just don't like my hair blowing into my mouth while I'm trying to eat."

"Understandable."

Henri arrived with the wine, along with Patricia, who set up an ice bucket in a stand next to the table.

Henri showed Deacon the label. It was pretty dark, and Deacon couldn't really read it. But he decided to trust the waiter wasn't substituting an inferior bottle.

At Deacon's nod, Henri opened it with a flourish, pouring a small amount into Deacon's glass. Deacon offered the taste to Callie, but she waved him off. So he did the honors. It tasted fine to him.

"Good," he said to Henri, who seemed inordinately pleased that the wine hadn't gone off.

Henri poured some for Callie, then filled Deacon's glass.

As Henri and Patricia left the table, Deacon raised his glass.

"To a beautiful woman, on a beautiful night." As he finished the toast, the wind suddenly gusted, and a splatter of rain hit the deck's roof.

Callie glanced above them at the worsening weather. "I'm not quite sure how to take the comparison."

"To a beautiful woman, on a not-so-beautiful night?" he tried.

"That works." She touched her glass to his, and they both drank.

"Oh, that's good." She kept her glass aloft, gazing at the wine inside.

His second taste was more impressive too. He had to admit, it was a very fine-tasting wine.

"Nice choice," she said.

"Thank you." He pretended there'd been some level of knowledge behind it.

Henri appeared again. "Excuse me, ma'am."

Callie tipped her head to look at him. "Yes?"

"The gentleman over there." Henri pointed. "Would like to buy your wine tonight."

Annoyance flared in Deacon. He looked past the waiter to the table Henri had indicated.

It was the Mayor. Hank Watkins was going to buy Callie a drink? Deacon didn't think so.

He set his napkin on the table, rising from his chair.

"The wine stays on my bill," he told the waiter as he passed.

Then he crossed the patio to Hank and his party of four businessmen.

"Deacon Holt, isn't it?" Hank asked heartily as he arrived.

"I know you consider yourself a bigshot around here," Deacon said to Hank, keeping his voice low, ignoring everyone else at the table. "But where I come from, you don't buy a woman a drink when she's with another man."

Hank squared his shoulders, setting his beefy hands on the tablecloth. "I'm only being neighborly, sir."

Deacon leaned slightly forward, keeping his gaze locked on Hank's. "And I'm being neighborly by telling you plain. Back off."

"Touchy?"

"You don't know the half of it."

Henri arrived, looking concerned. "Mayor? Mr. Holt?"

"It's fine, Henri," Hank said. "Mr. Holt was just leaving."

"So long as we're clear," Deacon said, hardening his gaze.

"I believe you've been perfectly clear." Hank gave a practiced smile to the rest of his party. "Mr. Holt prefers to take care of his own bill."

"Indeed, he does," Deacon said. He straightened and turned away.

Back at the table, Callie looked puzzled. "Is everything okay?"

"It is now." He sat down and repositioned his napkin.

"Why did Hank want to pay for the wine?"

"It was a power play. It had nothing to do with the wine."

She looked confused.

"He wanted to impress you by proving he's rich."

Now she looked amused. "By paying for a bottle of *wine*?" She lifted her glass. "Exactly how much did this cost?"

"Seven-hundred dollars."

Her expression fell. The glass slipped from her fingers, bouncing on the table.

She gasped, while Deacon reached for the glass, saving it before it could roll into her lap.

She stared at the widening, wet circle in horror. "I just spilled a hundred dollars' worth of wine."

"Good thing it was white."

"*Deacon*. What were you thinking?"

"About what?" He used his napkin to blot the spill.

"Spending so much money?"

"I thought it would be good. And it was good. It *is* good. Don't worry about the price."

"How can I not worry about the price?"

"I can afford it," he said. "I can easily afford it."

It was true. Just because he didn't choose to spend his money on luxury items, didn't mean he couldn't afford to buy them.

Alex and Patricia bustled over to the table.

"We can move you to a new table," Alex said.

"It's fine," Callie said.

"If you're sure," Alex said.

Patricia blotted the spill, replaced Callie's wineglass and produced a new napkin for Deacon.

In the blink of an eye, the table was almost back to normal.

Henri joined the trope. "Is there anything I can do to help?"

Callie started to giggle.

Henri raised his brow, looking concerned.

"We're really not batting a thousand on this, are we?" she said to Deacon.

He felt himself relax. He could see the humor in the situation, and he chuckled along with her. "But we do keep getting up to bat."

"You have to admire that about us."

Henri looked from one to the other. He didn't seem to know what to say.

"I think Mrs. Clarkson might like some more wine," Deacon said.

"Indeed, she would." Callie held up her glass.

"Of course," Henri quickly answered, gesturing to the bottle.

Patricia retrieved it from the ice bucket, dried it and poured.

"I can take your order whenever you're ready," Henri said, seeming to recover his poise.

"Give us a few minutes," Deacon said.

As Henri withdrew, Deacon raised his glass again. "To…?"

There was a spark of mischief in her eyes as she put her glass to his. "To a slightly crazy man, on a slightly crazy night."

"I'll drink to that."

* * *

“You have to tell me about last night.” Hannah sidled up to Callie at the front counter.

It was the late-morning lull, and Callie was refilling the coffee-bean dispensers.

“I had a good time,” Callie said, feeling a warm surge of emotion at the memories: laughing over dinner, then walking along the river path, Deacon’s jacket draped around her shoulders against the cold.

“You gotta give me more than that.” There was a thread of laughter in Hannah’s voice. “I like the way your eyes are shining. So, did you…”

Callie glanced up from her work and immediately understood Hannah’s meaning. “No, we didn’t.”

“Too bad. Why not?”

“It didn’t seem… I don’t know. It wasn’t what I expected. He wasn’t what I expected.”

Deacon had called her a cab. His good-night kiss was passionate and wonderful, and it lasted a very long time. But he hadn’t suggested anything more.

Hannah’s enthusiasm dimmed. “Oh. Not so good, then?”

“Not *not* good. More…” Callie searched for the words. “Intriguing, maybe. It’s like he’s got this polished thing going on at the surface, but you break through and he’s super down to earth. He’s got a good sense of humor. He seems smart.”

Hannah cocked her head. “I’m not hearing any good reason to hold back.”

“I’m not holding back. I wasn’t holding back.” Callie hadn’t made any overt sexual moves, but she hadn’t been standoffish either.

“He’s holding back? That seems odd. I mean, for a guy.”

The bell on the door tinkled, and Hannah looked in that direction.

"Oh, heads up," she said.

Callie looked, her chest contracting with the expectation of seeing Deacon. It had only been twelve hours, but she was more than ready to see him again.

But it was Hank who walked in.

"I got this," Hannah said, stepping up to the counter.

Disappointed, Callie went back to scooping varieties of coffee beans into the glass cylinder dispensers.

"Hello, Hank," Hannah said behind her.

"Good morning, Hannah."

"What can I get for you today?"

"A cappuccino and one of those chocolate-dipped shortbreads."

"You got it." Hannah rang up the order.

"And, Hannah?"

"Yes?" There was an expectant lilt in her voice.

"Can you ask Callie if she has a moment to talk?"

Hannah paused for a second. "Sure."

You had to be looking for it, but Callie caught the disappointment in Hannah's response. Hannah was such a fun, compassionate and beautiful woman, and Hank had never been married. Callie didn't understand why he couldn't seem to see the potential for the two of them.

Hannah turned. "Callie?"

Callie pretended she hadn't been paying any attention to the conversation. She glanced over her shoulder. "Yes?"

"The Mayor wants to talk to you."

"Sure." She washed her hands and dried them on a towel.

Hank had moved partway down the counter while

Hannah worked on the cappuccino, so Callie followed him there.

"I won't ask you to sit down," Hank said.

She was relieved. "We are pretty busy today."

She would rather keep Hank at arm's length.

She might agree with Frederick on the wisdom of having a cordial relationship with the city's politicians. But getting too close was inviting trouble. And Hank had been unusually friendly the past few weeks.

She'd already joined a committee and been a party to a donation. She didn't want to be drawn any further into any political web.

"I can see that," Hank said. "I just wanted to make sure there was no misunderstanding."

She could only assume he was talking about the building permit for the deck. As far as she knew, everything was in order.

"My gesture at dinner last night, it was meant to be friendly and welcoming, nothing more. I fear Deacon Holt misconstrued my motives. I don't want you to think badly of me."

The unexpected turn of the conversation surprised her. "I don't think badly of you."

Even if Deacon was right, and Hank had been showing off that he was rich, she wasn't going to worry about it. It seemed unlikely Hank had known the price of the wine. In fact, it would be odd if he had. In which case, Hank's version was the more plausible. He was trying to be welcoming to a potential city investor.

"I'm very glad to hear that," Hank said. "Will you be at the meeting Thursday?"

Callie wished she could skip it. But she'd promised herself she was joining the City Beautification Committee for more than just her permit. It was how she'd soothed her conscience. She wasn't about to stop attending now that she had her permit in hand.

"I'll be there," she said.

"Good. That's good. You should know there's talk of putting a rose garden and a water feature at Fifth and Bay Street."

It took Callie a moment to picture it in her mind. "Do you mean blocking off the through traffic?"

"Traffic would reroute on Balsam Crescent."

"But…" A feeling of dread slid through her. "Whose idea was that?"

Blocking off Bay Street would significantly impact traffic flow to Downright Sweet. They'd stand to lose a huge percentage of their tourist business.

"I'm looking into it," Hank said, concern clear in his expression. "Can I get back to you?"

"Yes, please do."

Hannah broke into the conversation. "Your order is ready, Hank."

Hank put his public smile back on as he turned to Hannah. "Thank you so much, Hannah. You're a treasure."

Hannah looked pleased by the compliment.

Callie was still absorbing the news. She counted on impulse purchases from the passing tourist traffic. Her local customers were a stalwart base to her business, but Downright Sweet couldn't survive without the money they made from tourists in the summer months to offset losses over the winter.

Frederick hadn't had life insurance. His health condition had made premiums far too expensive. And they'd spent all they had buying the house and the bakery.

He'd once told her he'd donated significantly to charities before they'd met. He'd said he regretted that decision. At the time, he'd never expected to have a family to support. She never imagined she'd someday be sorry he'd donated.

But what was done, was done. Now she needed the bakery to be profitable. She had the boys' education to worry about, upkeep on the house and day-to-day living expenses.

"Something's wrong," Hannah muttered to her as Hank chose a table.

"Nothing huge." She sure didn't want to worry Hannah.

"What is it? What did Hank want?"

"It's the beautification committee. Some of their ideas are pretty out there."

"That's because they're all geriatrics with short-term memory loss. Well, except for you and Hank, of course," Hannah hastily added.

"I am definitely going to have to keep attending those meetings."

Beautification was one thing. But the city's economy was important, too. If the committee's decisions started impacting businesses, everyone was going to suffer.

"Maybe Deacon will come with you."

"Maybe."

The meetings would definitely be more fun if Deacon came along. And perhaps he'd be willing to lend a voice of sanity. His transportation business wouldn't need property in the downtown core. But if he was planning to live here, he'd probably care about the overall success of the city. Maybe he'd be willing to side with her.

"And then, after the meeting..." Hannah let her voice trail off meaningfully.

Callie rolled her eyes. "You have a one-track mind."

"You should have a one-track mind, too. You're dating a hunky guy, and your level of sexual deprivation has got to be off the charts."

"Hannah!"

"I'm just calling it like it is."

"That's not *like it is.*" Callie didn't have a one-track mind. She wasn't obsessed with sex. Okay, she was a little obsessed with Deacon. And she'd like to have sex with Deacon. And she did think about that an awful lot.

But she wouldn't say she had a one-track mind.

She thought about other things.

A little bit.

Sometimes.

Deacon accepted the video conference call from Tyrell, bringing the man's face up on the tablet screen in the hotel suite. Tyrell was obviously in his office.

"I need an update," Tyrell said without preamble.

"I'm here. I've met her. I'm making progress."

"What kind of progress?"

"The getting-to-know-her kind of progress." Deacon wasn't about to share anything personal with Tyrell.

"I heard you went on a date."

"What do you mean, you heard?"

Who would Tyrell have heard from? Did Tyrell have contacts in Charleston?

"Are you spying on me?" Deacon demanded, rocking back in his desk chair.

"Of course I'm spying on you. I don't trust you. And I need to know what's going on down there."

"Then ask your spies."

"My spies weren't on the date. And they're not inside her house. What's going on with the Mayor?"

Deacon told himself not to be surprised by Tyrell's behavior.

"I don't exactly know," Deacon answered honestly. He'd been giving a lot of thought to the Mayor. "Hank is definitely interested in Callie. I can't tell for sure if she has any interest in him."

Deacon couldn't definitively say she wasn't. Hank was quite a bit older than her. But it was possible she was drawn to political power. It was an explanation that had been rolling around in Deacon's head.

"Get her interested in *you*," Tyrell said.

"I'm *trying*." Deacon found it easy to get annoyed with Tyrell. "I'm succeeding. I think."

Callie had seemed to enjoy their date.

Deacon had been the one to stop at a good-night kiss. It wasn't like she'd pushed him away. In the moment, he'd thought taking it slow was the best decision. But he was only guessing at that, as well.

"You've met my grandsons." Tyrell's words weren't a question.

"A couple of times. I don't know if you've seen pictures—"

"I've seen pictures."

"Then you know they're Aaron and Beau 2.0."

Tyrell gave a genuine smile.

Deacon wasn't sure he'd seen that before. "What can you tell me about Frederick's trust fund?"

"What do you want to know?"

"How much was in it? Ballpark?"

"Enough. Millions. Why?"

The answer hit on the heart of Deacon's confusion. "Because Callie doesn't act like a woman with money."

"Oh, she's got money all right."

Deacon tapped his index finger on the desktop. "Why doesn't she want me to know she has money?"

"Did you mess up? Does she think you're a gold digger?"

"I didn't mess anything up. I've done everything in my power to prove to her that *I* have money. I pointed her at Mobi Transportation. I've upgraded my wardrobe, my accessories. I've got the most expensive hotel suite in town, a high-end car. There's no way she thinks I need money."

"Well, you better figure it out."

"I am going to figure it out. Millions, you say?" Deacon's brain went back over the bakery oven conversation. It didn't make any sense.

"She was a waif when Frederick found her," Tyrell said.

"That's what she told me."

"It worked for her once."

"So you think she's playing the part of the damsel in distress."

"Yes. Go rescue her, Deacon. Time's a wasting."

Tyrell's theory didn't feel right to Deacon. But he didn't have a better one, and something was definitely up with Callie and money.

"And get that mayor out of the picture," Tyrell demanded.

"I'm working on it."

"Work harder. My people tell me she's with him right now."

"She's *what*?" Deacon glanced at his watch. It was only five fifteen.

On Mondays, Callie didn't leave the bakery until six thirty.

"They just left the bakery together."

"I'm on it." Deacon signed off the call, grabbed his wallet and phone and left the hotel.

It was a short walk to the bakery, and he was there

in minutes, looking up and down the street for signs of Callie.

It didn't take him long to find her. She and Hank were at a table on the patio of a nearby café. They sat side by side, heads close together, intense emotion in their expressions.

Callie was upset about something.

Hank seemed to be comforting her.

He took her hand.

She shook her head.

He spoke at length, clearly trying to talk her into something.

Deacon took two steps forward before stopping himself.

What could he say? What could he do? What was she up to?

She raised her head, and Deacon quickly stepped back, shielding himself from her view with an oak tree.

Then she nodded, and Hank squeezed her hands with his. Hank smiled, and Deacon wanted to punch him in the teeth.

Deacon acknowledged the danger in his reaction. He should be frustrated that he had competition from the Mayor. But he shouldn't be jealous. It shouldn't hit him on an emotional level.

Callie was a means to an end. She was a complicated woman, who obviously had an agenda of her own. He needed to harness that. He needed to use it by pursuing their relationship. But he also needed to stay detached.

The smart play was to coolly and dispassionately focus her attention on him, instead of Hank. Whatever Hank could do, Deacon would do better. That meant eliminating the differences between them.

He pulled his phone from his pocket and dialed Tyrell.

"Yes?" Tyrell answered in a gruff tone.

"It's Deacon."

"I know."

Deacon could hear male voices in the background. "Can you talk?"

"Give me a minute."

It went silent.

"What is it?" Tyrell asked.

"I need a political future."

"Explain."

"It needs to be something convincing, maybe a shot at the state legislature. I want Callie to believe there's a powerful political career in my future. Who do you know who can help?"

"Everyone."

"Okay, who do you trust?"

Tyrell was silent for a minute. "Senator Cathers."

"Seriously?" Deacon couldn't help but be impressed. Senator Cathers was the Senior Senator from Virginia.

"He's speaking at a Chamber of Commerce event in Richmond tomorrow. I'll have him mention your name."

It took Deacon a second to respond. Just like that, Tyrell could put words in a Senator's mouth?

"Make sure you record it," Tyrell continued. "Figure out a way to put it in front of her. Yada, yada."

"Yeah, I get it. I get it."

"Good."

Deacon glanced back at Callie and Hank. Every instinct he had told him to march up to the table and drag the two of them apart. But he had to be smart about this. He had to be methodical. He had to make her come willingly to him.

Five

Callie left the City Beautification Committee meeting, anger propelling her forward. She made it through the door and halfway across the porch before she heard Hank's voice.

"Callie, wait."

She ignored him and kept walking.

"Stop." His hand clasped around her upper arm.

"Let go of me." She tried to shake him off.

"Just listen for a minute."

"Listen?" she demanded, rounding on him. "I *have* listened. I listened really good back there while you threw me and Downright Sweet under the bus. I didn't ask you for anything, but you promised to support me."

If she'd known what he was going to do, she could have been better prepared.

"There was nothing I could say to them that would have made a difference," he said.

"You didn't even try. Never mind try, you jumped on the bandwagon with the other side."

They hadn't formally voted on the rose garden tonight, but it was only a matter of time until they did. It would pass, and her business was going to suffer. She was going to lose money. She couldn't afford to operate at a loss, and Hank knew that.

"This is only the first round," he said.

"No, Hank. This was a knockout punch. There's nobody on my side. Everyone loves the rose garden proposal. Nice PowerPoint by the way."

"You have to look at the long game, Callie."

"There's no long game. There's no game. There's only the demise of Downright Sweet."

"You're getting hysterical."

"No. I'm getting angry."

"Please calm down." His patronizing tone was offensive.

"I'm leaving." She looked pointedly at where he held her arm.

He let go of her arm but took her hand. "I know what it is you need."

Why did he insist on touching her so much? It was really annoying. But his grip was firm enough that she couldn't easily slip out of it.

"It's hardly a secret," she said.

"What I mean is I know how to help you."

"You didn't help me." When she'd needed his help, he'd sat mute in the committee.

He seemed to gather his thoughts. "This is going to sound bold, but I think there's a way we can help each other."

She wanted to jerk her hands from his. Every instinct she had told her to ignore Frederick's advice and walk away. Being friendly to the Mayor wasn't helping her one little bit.

"You're an incredibly beautiful woman, Callie."

His words took her by surprise. "What's that got to do with—"

"Let me rephrase," he rushed on. "You're a wonderful woman. And your boys, well, I think they're terrific."

Unnerved, she searched his expression. Was he threatening her boys?

He eased a little closer, lowering his voice. "You and I, Callie. We should think seriously about teaming up."

"What do you mean?" But she was afraid that she knew exactly what he meant.

"I'm saying that I'm attracted to you."

Something shriveled inside her.

"I'm more than just attracted to you," he continued.

She'd always considered him a fairly distinguished man. But she'd never had a single romantic thought about him.

"You, me, a perfect little family…think of the possibilities."

Forget Frederick's advice. She jerked her hand free of Hank's.

"Nobody knows this yet." He talked faster. "But I'm running for Governor next election."

She couldn't think of a single response.

Should she have seen this coming?

He'd been friendly, sure. But he was friendly to everyone. She'd never given him the slightest cause to think she was romantically interested in him.

His enthusiasm was obvious. "I have dozens of well-placed supporters. Contributions are pouring in. Our future would be—"

"I can't," she blurted out.

What had she ever done to make him think she'd be swayed by his political aspirations?

He took a moment. "Is it the age difference?"

"Yes." It seemed like the simplest answer. It was the age difference and so much more.

"There are a few years between us, I know. But it happens all the time."

"Hank, please stop. I'm sorry." She didn't know why she was apologizing. She only knew she wanted out of this conversation.

"You're a practical woman, Callie. It made sense for you to marry Frederick when you needed him, and it makes sense for you to marry me now."

There was no comparison between Hank and Frederick—none at all.

"You and your sons will have everything you could ever want."

"This isn't going to happen, Hank."

His gaze narrowed. It seemed like his patience was wearing thin. "You've considered it for all of two minutes."

"It's not something I'm—"

"Is that all I get? A whole two minutes of your time?"

She didn't know what to say that wouldn't make the situation worse.

His voice took on a harder edge. "The rose garden would get out of your way." He snapped his fingers in the air. "Just like that. Gone. I can do that. I can fix things."

"You think I'd marry you to move a rose garden?" The idea was both preposterous and revolting.

"It's not just the rose garden. That's small time. I'm talking about the Governor's mansion, Callie."

She took a small step back. Like there was a house in the world that would entice her to marry him.

His voice turned gravelly, his expression darkening. “I make a much better ally than an adversary.”

A chill ran through her, and she realized she might be better off with another tactic. She forced herself to lighten her tone. “Hank, I’m flattered. But you have to know this is very sudden.”

The words seemed to mollify him, and he gave a thoughtful nod. “Fair enough. You need to think about it. I can understand that.”

“I’ll think about it.” She would. But not in the way he meant.

She wanted to appease him for the moment, to put an end to the drama. She wanted out of this conversation and to go home to her boys.

Luckily, three people chose that moment to exit the main door and join them on the porch.

Callie took advantage of the distraction. “Good night, Hank.”

She trotted down the stairs and walked quickly to the sidewalk, resisting the urge to break into a sprint. She wanted to leave Hank far, far behind.

She made it fifty yards.

“Whoa,” came a voice from the street side.

It took her a second to realize it was Deacon. Her heart was beating fast, and she was breathing deeply.

“Where’s the fire?” he asked.

She ordered herself to pull it together as she looked over at him. “You missed the meeting.”

He fell into step beside her. “I was hoping to catch the tail end. How did it go?”

“Not great.”

“No? What happened?”

She opened her mouth. Then she hesitated, unsure of how much to share.

* * *

Deacon had felt an immediate lift in his mood when he spotted Callie.

She had energy. She sparkled. The air seemed lighter around her, the world a more interesting place.

If something had gone wrong for her, he wanted to help.

"Tell me?" he prompted.

"Everyone *loves* that rose garden," she said, her sarcasm crystal clear.

Deacon had heard about the garden, and he knew it was going to be a big problem for Callie.

"What about Lawrence?" he asked. As far as Deacon was concerned, Lawrence owed Callie his loyalty.

"Lawrence and Hank put on a PowerPoint together. It swayed everyone who might have been on the fence."

"I'm really sorry to hear that." Deacon impulsively took her hand as they walked along the edge of the park.

It felt good. It felt ridiculously natural to be connected to her.

At the same time, it was disturbing to learn that Lawrence had abandoned her. Could Lawrence be naïve about politics? Or maybe two-thousand dollars didn't buy much goodwill these days.

"They didn't vote yet," she said. "But it would have been seven to one if they had."

Deacon looked for a way to help. "What's your next move?"

A pained expression came over her face.

"Is there more?" he asked.

It took her a second to answer. "No. Not exactly." Then she rushed on. "I don't know *what* to do next. All I want to do is run a business, a simple little bakery that gives people tasty treats. I don't want political intrigue.

I don't want favors and tactics and counter-schemes." She abruptly stopped and turned to face him. "Is that so much to ask?"

"No." His answer was simple.

And she was beautiful in the moonlight.

He smoothed her windblown hair. "How can I help?"

"You're listening to me complain. That's a help."

"I'm happy to do it. But it's not very practical."

"Hank's offered to help." There was an odd inflection in her voice.

Deacon's hackles rose. He didn't want Hank anywhere near Callie's problems.

"How?" Deacon asked, his question clipped and short. Too late, he wished he'd been more careful with his tone.

But Callie didn't seem to notice. She gave a dismissive wave with her free hand and started walking again. "He wasn't any help tonight, that's for sure."

Deacon wanted to press, but he also wanted to move past the topic of Hank.

"What about you making a donation?" he asked, watching for her reaction to the suggestion. With this much at stake, would she finally admit to having money?

"Even if I could afford it, I'm not going down that road."

"There's no way for you to come up with the money?" He covertly watched her expression.

"No. I'm not taking out a loan against my business to bribe a city politician. Wow. That sounds really unsavory, doesn't it?" Her expression was inscrutable.

He knew she was lying about the money. She could be faking the moral outrage, as well. She seemed completely genuine, but he had to be smart about this.

"Can I ask you a question?" he asked.

She hesitated. "You can."

"It's about Frederick."

"I don't mind talking about Frederick."

Deacon weighed the pros and cons in his mind. "Were you in love with him?"

Callie slipped her hand from Deacon's hold, and he could have kicked himself.

They walked in silence for a several minutes, passing the end of the park and turning onto a residential street.

He was about to apologize, when she spoke.

"It was complicated," she said. "I was young. I'd been through a lot. My family was severely dysfunctional. My mother died, and I was all alone in the world with nothing. I'd already dropped out of high school. I could barely keep a roof over my head. And Frederick was kind. He wanted children. And I, well, I wanted security. We each wanted something the other could provide. Frederick was a decent man. I respected him. And I liked him."

She made it sound almost noble, marrying a handicapped man for his money to give him children.

"I don't regret it," she said.

The cynical part of Deacon wondered why she would. She had two boys she clearly loved, all of Frederick's money, and she was free to embark on a new relationship and better her circumstance even more.

He shouldn't care. He didn't care. It wasn't like she was robbing banks. And her pragmatic attitude suited his purposes. All he had to do was make sure he was the next rich husband on her list.

"I understand," he said.

She paused once again, turning toward him. "Do you?"

He took both her hands in his, happy to pretend he was buying the image she projected. "You're kind. You're generous. You're devoted, a paragon really." It wasn't hard for him to say those words. He believed them.

She smiled with self-deprecating humor. "That's ridiculous. You should see what goes on inside my head."

"I'd like to," he said, moving in. "I'd love to hear your innermost thoughts."

That wasn't the only thing he'd love. His gaze focused on her lips, dark and soft under the faraway streetlight.

"Deacon," she sighed, her eyes fluttering closed.

He cradled her cheek with one hand, leaned forward and kissed her soft mouth.

He instantly stopped caring who was pretending and who was playacting. It didn't matter. Nothing mattered except the taste of Callie.

"Come in," she whispered against his lips.

It took a moment for her words to penetrate, and he realized they were in front of her house.

"You're sure?" he asked, not wanting to seem too eager.

"I'm sure."

He held her hand as they took the walkway and entered the house.

There, Pam said a breezy good-night before she limped to her car.

"She's off the crutches," Deacon noted, moving closer to Callie in the living room.

"The sprain is healing fast."

"That's good." He couldn't stop himself from touching Callie, so he brushed her shoulder.

The fabric of her simple T-shirt was thin, and he could feel her warmth on his fingertips.

"A drink?" she asked, the slightest quaver to her voice.

"Whatever you're having." He kissed her temple.

She stood still for the length of the kiss.

Then she turned toward him and tipped her chin. "I think I'm having you."

As her words hit his brain, the world disappeared. Passion obliterated everything.

"You are incredible," he whispered as he drew her into his arms, kissing her mouth, slanting his head to deepen the kiss. Her taste filled his senses.

He pressed her fast against him, sliding his palms down her back, reveling in the tone of her body, the indentation of her waist, then the flare of her hips and her rear.

He held her close, his arousal building.

She moaned in response, the sound vibrating against his lips.

His hands convulsed against her.

"Upstairs," she whispered.

He didn't need another invitation. He scooped her into his arms and headed for the staircase.

"Right," she said. "End of the hall."

He walked as fast as he dared, and in seconds they were through the double doors, into an ornate, cream-toned bedroom with a fireplace and a massive canopy bed. It was lit by a small Tiffany lamp on the dresser. Impatience screeched inside his head.

Instead, he set her on her feet. His hands all but trembling, he cradled her face. He kissed her tenderly, ordering himself to take it slow and gentle. She'd never done this before.

Her hands went to the buttons on his shirt. They were trembling.

"Are you okay?" he asked, worried he'd frightened her.

"Huh?" She looked up at him, her blue-green eyes glazed in the dim light.

"You're hands are shaking."

"Help me," she said.

It took him a second to realize she meant with his buttons.

"I can't get them." She looked at one of her hands. "Is this normal?"

"Are you afraid?"

"What? No. *No.* I'm… I don't know what I am. But could you please take off your clothes?"

"Yes, ma'am." He practically ripped his buttons open.

While he did that, she peeled her T-shirt over her head, revealing a lacy white bra. It was irresistible. She was irresistible.

She pulled off her slacks and stood in front of him in equally tempting panties, wispy and lacy, minuscule and sheer.

"Deacon?" she asked.

He gave himself a shake. "Yeah?"

"You're overdressed."

"I'm in awe." He drew her toward him, wrapping his arms around her, feeling her melt into him. "You are stunningly beautiful."

"You might be, too," she said, pushing his shirt off his shoulders. "But I can't tell yet."

He chuckled, half at himself and half at her. She wasn't anywhere near what he'd expected.

He quickly stripped to his black boxers.

"That's nice," she said, gazing at him, reaching out to stroke his chest.

Her fingertips sent flares of passion across his skin. He closed his eyes, arousal hammering along every nerve. Her hand moved lower and lower, until he grabbed it to stop her.

"Pace yourself," he rasped. "Pace me," he corrected.

He wrapped one arm around her waist, and with the other hand, he covered her breast.

She gasped, and when he kissed her mouth, she met his tongue, tangling with it.

He unhooked her bra, sliding it away to touch her skin, skimming his knuckles over her nipple, drawing it between his thumb and forefinger, watching in satisfaction as her head tipped back, her eyes closed, and her mouth dropped open.

He settled her gently on the bed, lay down beside her.

"Let me," he whispered, using his hands and his lips to kiss and caress her, finding her sensitive spots, doing his utmost to bring her to a perfect arousal.

She touched him back, exploring his body, testing his concentration and his resolve.

When her hand wrapped around him, he spun her onto her back, knowing he was beyond his limit.

He looked deep into her eyes. "Now?"

She nodded.

He was quick with a condom, and then he was above her. Her legs went around him, and he slid them to a slow and perfect meld.

Her eyes were wide, her cheeks flushed, and her lips formed a perfect *oh*.

"Good?" he asked her, loving the expression on her face.

"Oh, Deacon."

"I know." He cupped her breast again, touching her nipple, bringing it to a peak.

He withdrew and surged, withdrew and surged.

Her fingertips grasped his shoulders, clinging tightly.

"What?" she gasped. "What do I…?"

"Nothing," he told her. "You're perfect. You're amazing. You're wonderful. Just let go." He kissed her deeply, canted her hips toward him, pressed deep, pulled back, feeling her body, listening to her sounds, guessing what made her feel best.

Her chopped moans guided him. He increased his pace, driving harder and harder. Insistent waves of pleasure drove deep in his abdomen. He lost his focus, lost control, lost his very mind.

Then she cried out his name, and he tumbled with her, wave after wave after wave of infinite pleasure washing through him and over him and all around him.

When he came back to earth, she was panting in his ear.

He eased his weight from her, giving her lungs some space.

"You okay?" he asked between his own gasps.

"Wow."

"Is that a good *wow*?"

She seemed to blink him into focus. "Wow. So that's what people were talking about."

He struggled not to laugh. But her expression was amazing, endearing and funny all at the same time.

He turned them together, putting her on top, wrapping himself around her and wishing he never had to let go.

He didn't know what to say. He couldn't find any words. So he stroked her hair and whispered her name, while her body went lax on top of him.

Callie woke up alone. The ceiling fan was whirring above her head. Two windows were open, and she was buried in a comforter, in the middle of the big bed.

She threw off the blanket, squelching her disappointment that Deacon had left while she was sleeping. Last night had been nothing short of magical. He was passionate, attentive and so incredibly sexy. Whatever happened between them after this, she would never regret making love with him.

It was bright in the room, brighter than normal. She glanced at her clock, shocked to see that it was nearly nine. The boys never slept this late.

She sat upright, worried something was wrong.

But then she heard their voices.

Ethan laughed, while James whooped.

Then she heard another voice. Deacon. He hadn't gone home last night.

She dropped her head back down on the pillow. Instead of going home, he'd gotten up with her boys, letting her have a rare sleep-in. Could he have made himself any more perfect?

She brushed her teeth, pulled on a pair of exercise pants and a T-shirt and wandered downstairs.

The voices were coming from the kitchen, and she walked to the doorway to find Deacon and the boys clustered around the stove. James was on the step stool, Ethan on a chair, while Deacon wielded a spatula in one hand. The kitchen counter was a mess of bowls and utensils and baking ingredients.

James spotted her first. "Deacon's making pancakes. They're shaped like race cars."

"Zoom cars, Mommy," Ethan called out.

Deacon turned with a smile. "Morning."

"Morning," she said, walking barefoot into the room. "Looks like you've been busy."

He glanced around the room, and his smile dimmed a little. "Won't take long to clean it up."

"Smells good," she said, realizing she should be appreciating his efforts, not criticizing them.

"They're banana," James said.

"And tasty syrup," Ethan sang out.

"I'm guessing that's a quote," she asked Deacon.

"Tasty syrup is the very best kind of syrup." He carefully flipped a pancake. "We're going to need plates."

James started to hop down.

"I'll get them," Callie said. "Can you get forks and knives?" she asked James.

"Wheels," Ethan announced, pointing to the pan.

Callie noticed Deacon was using a back burner, and the position of Ethan's chair made it impossible for him to reach the hot surface. More points for Deacon.

She set four plates out on the table, while James carefully arranged the cutlery. She added butter, syrup and juice to the mix. Then she started the coffee maker.

"I hope we're not keeping you from something," she said to Deacon.

He reached along the counter and wrapped his hand around her forearm, urging her closer, while leaning in, speaking in an undertone. "There's nowhere else I want to be."

After a quick glance to make sure the boys weren't watching, he gave her a tender kiss.

She smiled, her heart feeling light.

"Pancakes one and two are ready for eating," he announced to the boys.

James put his arms out like wings and made an engine noise as he trotted to the table. Deacon wrapped an arm around Ethan's waist, making a matching noise as he swooped Ethan to the table, settling him in his booster seat.

He took their plates to the stove and placed an impressively shaped car pancake on each of them.

"Where did you learn to do that?" Callie asked.

"My mom was creative."

"I can see that." She spread some butter on Ethan's pancake and added a drizzle of syrup.

"Any requests?" Deacon asked her.

She didn't understand the question.

"What shape do you want your pancake?"

She smiled as she cut Ethan's car into careful squares. "Round is fine for me."

"I'm going to need more information," Deacon said.

"You need me to explain round?"

"Do you want an orange, a beach ball, the moon? You're going to have to be specific."

"Get the moon, Mommy. Get the moon," James called.

She couldn't help laughing. "I'll take the moon."

"One moon, coming up."

"What are you having?" she asked, moving to stand beside him at the stove.

"I'm going with a base drum."

"You must be hungry."

"I am." He paused. "I worked up an appetite last night."

Her cheeks grew warm. "Yeah." She didn't know what else to say.

"Don't tell me you're feeling shy."

"A little," she admitted. She'd never had breakfast with a lover before. She had to wonder if children were often part of the equation.

"You should feel great. I feel great." Deacon put a hand on her shoulder. "You're amazing."

"You're pretty amazing yourself."

She could see him smile out of the corner of her eye.

"Any chance you can take the day off?" he asked.

She hesitated. She wasn't sure she wanted to hop immediately back into bed. Well, part of her did. But part of her wanted to take a breath.

Deacon must have guessed the direction of her thoughts, because he nudged her playfully with his hip. "I thought we could take the boys to the beach."

"Oh, uh, let me check with Hannah."

"I didn't mean *that.*" His tone was teasing.

"I know."

"Don't get me wrong. I'd do it again in a heartbeat. But that wasn't where I was going."

Her self-consciousness rose again. Then she told herself to quit being foolish. She wasn't some blushing teenager.

"Juice, Mommy, juice," Ethan called from the table, his little heels banging against the chair legs.

She stretched up to whisper in Deacon's ear. "I would too."

Then she sashayed across the room to pour the orange juice.

Deacon was right behind her with the pancakes.

He set them down and pulled out her chair. Then he leaned in behind her as she sat. "Teasing me?"

She gave him an unrepentant grin. "Just being honest."

His blue eyes twinkled in response.

"Anybody want to go to the beach today?" she asked the boys. She was confident Hannah wouldn't mind holding down the fort at the bakery.

"Beach," Ethan shouted.

"Can we build a sand castle?" James asked.

"We sure can," she said, cutting into her pancake.

"Castle," Ethan sang out.

"He doesn't seem as noisy when you're outside," Callie told Deacon.

"I don't mind. I get it. I was a boy once myself."

She took a bite of her pancake. It was delicious. "Secret recipe?"

"It's all yours if you want it."

"I do."

"Mommy, can I take my orange wagon?" James asked.

"I don't think the wheels will roll on the beach."

"They might."

"They might get stuck in the sand."

"Why do you want your wagon?" Deacon asked.

"It's big. It'll fit a whole mountain of sand." James made an expansive gesture with both hands.

"Watch your fork, honey." Callie could live without syrup drops flying through the kitchen.

"Do you have buckets?" Deacon asked James. "Your mom's right. The wagon wheels will probably get stuck. But I'm pretty strong, I can carry big buckets."

"Can we take the bubble tub?" James asked, his eyes wide with excitement.

"The bubble tub?" Deacon asked.

"It's a laundry tub. We play bubbles in it in the backyard."

Deacon lifted his brow to her in a question.

"I have to warn you, it's pretty big," she said on a laugh. She didn't imagine the beach would do it any harm.

"Done," Deacon said. "Let's see how much I can lift."

Six

Callie's sons were slightly sun-kissed, thoroughly exhausted and now sound asleep. Deacon gave one last look at Ethan in his crib and James in a sports car bed, still marveling at how much they looked like their uncles, Aaron and Beau. Then he followed Callie out of their bedroom.

"You wore them into the ground," she whispered to Deacon.

"They were the ones who did that to me." He'd been impressed at their energy levels all day long.

They'd slowed down around one o'clock, but half an hour of shade, a couple of hotdogs and some hydration, and they were ready to go all over again. They'd built a sandcastle, rented bikes, tossed a beach ball around and played endlessly in the waves, finding tiny shells and sea creatures.

"Should we eat something?" she asked.

"I don't know. Are we hungry?" He smoothed back her hair and kissed her neck, like he'd been dying to do for hours.

Her creamy, copper limbs and bare midriff had been teasing him all day long.

"You want to stay?" she asked, stopping at the top of the stairs and turning to face him.

"Do you mean overnight?" He didn't want to misunderstand.

"Yes, I mean overnight."

"Absolutely." He couldn't think of anything he'd rather do.

"Then, we can probably take time out to eat."

"I suppose I can wait."

"Yes, you can wait." Her tone was mock-stern. "It's barely eight o'clock."

"I can wait." In fact, he wanted to wait. He wanted to hang out with her in this big, comfy house, enjoy her company, have a little dinner, all the while anticipating that he would be holding her in his arms, making love with her, sleeping curled around her lithe body.

"I can order something in," he offered as they started down the stairs.

"There are leftover pancakes."

"You've been living in mom-world way too long."

She grinned over her shoulder.

"I was thinking of braised duckling and wild mushrooms," he said.

"You can get that delivered?"

"You can get anything delivered. They'll throw in salad, wine and dessert."

"I leave it in your capable hands."

He gave her a mock salute. "On it, ma'am."

"I'll pick up the toys."

He gazed around the jumble of the living room. He didn't mind the lived-in look, but he knew Callie was more comfortable when things were tidy.

"I'll help in a minute," he told her, borrowing her tablet and bringing up a food delivery app.

It was quick and painless to place the order. And then, though he preferred to stay with her in the fantasy and forget about the outside world, he did his duty and set the tablet to a Virginia political news page.

"We've got thirty minutes," he told her, placing the tablet on the coffee table.

"No," she said, seeming to randomly throw the word into the conversation, as she finished lining up stuffed bears across an armchair.

"No what?"

"No, we're not tearing our clothes off for thirty minutes, while we wait for dinner."

"Did I say that?" Not that he'd turn her down. He definitely wouldn't turn her down.

"It's in your eyes."

He moved toward her. "You haven't even looked in my eyes."

"Then it's in your tone."

He looped an arm around her waist. "The only thing in my tone is a desire to get you to sit down and stop working. You have to be just as tired as I am."

She let herself be led to the sofa. "I didn't carry anywhere near as much sand. And you had Ethan on your bike."

"He's not heavy." Truth was Deacon had been entertained by the little guy's chatter throughout the ride.

She sat at one end of the sofa, while he moved to the other to keep himself away from temptation. Because, despite his protests, he was having a very hard time keeping his hands off her. And it was time for him to focus on impressing her.

He pretended to bump the tablet as he sat down, lighting the page he'd queued up. He'd enlarged his name in the title of the article, hoping she'd notice.

She didn't, and the page soon went dark.

"Are you thirsty?" he asked, looking for another excuse to touch the tablet. "I ordered wine, but I can get you something while we wait."

"I'm fine."

"Well, I'd like some water." He rose, touched the tablet screen again, surreptitiously turning it her way. Then he headed into the kitchen.

"You sure I can't grab you one?" he called back.

"No, that's…okay, maybe, sure. Bring me one."

He took two bottles of water from the fridge door, breaking their seals as he returned.

Bingo. She was reading the article.

She looked up. "What's this?"

"Hmm?" He set a water bottle down close to her and took a drink from his own.

"It's about you."

"Me? Really?" He feigned surprise. "I must have typed my name in the wrong box. Is it the Mobi Transportation family picnic? I killed in the ring toss."

"No. It's Senator Cathers. He was talking about you."

Still pretending to be confused, Deacon reached for the tablet. "When?"

"At some event last week."

He scanned the article. "Oh, man. This is embarrassing. I told him not to do that."

"Is it true? Are you going into politics?" She didn't look particularly happy at the prospect.

"No. Well, maybe someday. There are a few people out there who think it's a good idea."

"For the power and influence?" she asked.

"To help my fellow Virginians." It was such a pat answer, it was almost laughable. But it was still the best answer. "There's a lot of work to be done in streamlining regulations, cutting red tape and creating jobs."

"Are you sure it's not for the power and influence?"

He lounged back, trying his best to look nonchalant. "That's not my focus at all. Why so skeptical?"

"I don't know."

He didn't buy it, and he wanted to get to the bottom of her thought processes. "Why?"

It took her a minute to answer. "I don't… It sure seems to be working for Hank Watkins."

Deacon tried to read her expression, but it was carefully neutral. For some reason, she was hiding her feelings about Hank's political power. Deacon couldn't tell which way to play this. So he waited.

She leaned forward and lifted her bottle of water, twisting off the cap and setting it down. "Hank says he can make the rose garden go away."

Deacon hid his reflexive annoyance. "He offered to fix your rose garden problem?"

"He did."

"Did you take him up on it?" Deacon hated the thought of Hank having leverage over her.

She frowned, her eyes hardening. "No."

"Good. I'll donate to the committee again." And this time, he'd make the donation big enough to make sure Lawrence stayed loyal.

"No," Callie said.

"What do you mean no? That's how we do an end run around Hank."

"It feels too much like bribery."

"It's not bribery. It's maybe, at most, gaining a little influence."

"You just said you didn't care about power and influence."

"I don't." What he cared about was helping Callie and disempowering Hank.

"Then why are you using it?"

"I'm not a politician, Callie." Deacon could see that he'd gone down the wrong path on that one, but it didn't mean he'd leave the field open for Hank to fix her problem.

"Not yet," she said.

"Maybe never. I'm a long, long way from a decision like that."

The doorbell rang.

She rose.

He stood with her. "I'll get that."

She nodded, looking sad and dejected. Their mood was completely ruined.

He moved to face her and took her hand. "I'm sorry."

"I am, too." Her eyes were wide and glassy.

"I won't make another donation."

"Thank you."

"Do you want me to leave?"

She hesitated. Then she slowly shook her head. "Stay."

He felt a huge weight come off his chest.

Callie had postponed long enough. It had been nearly a week since Hank had showed his true colors, and she owed it to Hannah to tell her the truth. The last staff member had just gone home for the evening, so it was only Callie and Hannah finishing the paperwork and calculating the day's bank deposit.

"You should get home to the boys," Hannah suggested as she sorted through the cash, putting it in neat stacks into the deposit bag.

Callie pulled a second chair up to the small round table in the compact office. There wasn't much room next to the bookshelf, so she leaned forward. "There's something I've been wanting to tell you," she opened.

Hannah smiled without looking up. "About a certain hunky tourist who's been hanging around every day, gazing at you like a lovesick calf?"

Callie didn't think that was a particularly accurate description of Deacon. But she was determined to stay on topic. "It's about Hank."

Hannah did look up. "Is something wrong? He hasn't been in for a few days. Did he catch that flu that's been going around?"

"It's not the flu."

"What is it? What's happened?"

"I saw him last Thursday, at the beautification committee meeting."

"Uh-huh."

"I didn't say anything to you then, but he went against me on the rose garden."

Hannah straightened a stack of twenties and put a band around them. "I'm sorry he did that. But maybe he had his reasons."

Callie slid a round mesh pencil holder over in front of her, absently separating the pens by color as she talked. "You really like him, don't you?"

"Everybody likes him. He's a great guy."

"Thing is." Callie put the four reds pens in a row. "He might not be such a great guy."

"Just because he's in favor of the rose garden?"

"I was mad about that. I admit it. But then…" Callie

drew out a black sharpie that didn't match anything else and tapped it on the table. "He said something, Hannah. I'm so sorry, but he…I guess…propositioned me."

Hannah's chin dropped.

Now that she'd broken the ice, Callie wanted to get it all out in the open. "He told me he was attracted to me. He said we could be a perfect little family, and if I agreed to be with him, the rose garden and all my other problems would go away."

Hannah swallowed. She seemed to be having trouble finding her voice. "What did you say?"

"I said *no*."

"Okay."

"I'm not interested in Hank." The only man Callie was interested in was Deacon.

She didn't want to insult Hannah by sharing her true feelings about Hank. She only wanted to stop Hannah from fantasizing about him. Hank was no good for Hannah. But Callie hated to hurt her friend's feelings.

Hannah began flipping through a stack of fives. "I sure called that one wrong, didn't I? Oh, well, what could I expect? The good ones always go for younger women."

Callie covered Hannah's hand with hers. "That's not always true. And Hank isn't one of the good ones."

"Just because he's attracted to you instead of me? That's perfectly normal. Look at you. You're extraordinary."

"I'm not extraordinary. I'm completely ordinary. And Hank was more interested in how the four of us would look as a family for his political career than he was in me personally. He doesn't even know me."

"Well, I know you," Hannah said with conviction. "And you are amazing."

"So are you. And you're beautiful. And any man

would be beyond lucky to date you. But it's not Hank. You're way too good for Hank."

"That doesn't seem to be the way Hank sees it."

"Hank's a fool."

A sheen came up in Hannah's eyes. "I'm the fool for thinking I had a shot."

Callie squeezed her hand, not sure what else to say.

"You should go home," Hannah told her. "James and Ethan will be waiting."

"I wish this hadn't happened," Callie said.

"Well, I'm glad it did. No point in an old woman like me pining for someone who's never even noticed her."

Callie smiled, hoping to lighten the mood. "You're not old. And you're not pining. You just had a misguided crush."

"Crushes are for high school."

"Crushes are for everybody. And you'll have another one. And it'll be soon. It's almost June, and the town's filling up with tourists, and new customers walk through that door every day. Heck, if Mobi Transport opens up a new terminal, the town may be crawling with single men."

Hannah cracked a smile. "You are an optimist."

"Not really." Callie was mostly a pessimist.

Before Frederick, her life had been a series of disasters and disappointments. She'd simply learned how to move forward in life, no matter what happened. A person could take a lot of hits and still get up.

Hannah went back to counting the cash. "I'll be fine. I'm glad I know. Thank you for telling me."

"Do you want to stop for a drink somewhere? We could grab something to eat." Callie had planned to meet Deacon after work for the sixth night in a row. But she was sure he'd understand if she cancelled.

"No thanks," Hannah said. "Do you mind if I take home a couple of the red velvet cupcakes?"

"Take as many as you need."

Hannah gave a brave smile. "Nothing a little buttercream won't fix. I'll see you tomorrow."

"If you're sure."

"I'm sure."

Callie's phone pinged with a text message.

"That'll be your hot guy," Hannah said.

Callie checked. Sure enough, it was Deacon. The message said he was out front waiting.

"Go do something wild," Hannah said. "I'm going to live vicariously through you for a few weeks."

"Something wild, huh?"

"Tell me all about it in the morning."

"If it's what you want, I will gladly share." Callie texted back to Deacon that she was on her way.

Then she logged out of her computer and headed through the dimmed dining room.

It felt good to see Deacon's face.

"What's wrong?" he asked, as she locked the door behind herself.

"Long day." She forced a smile. "I'm glad you're here."

He swung an arm over her shoulders. "I'm glad to be here."

They took a few steps along the sidewalk, but Deacon slowed, stopping.

"Tell me," he said.

"Tell you what?"

"Your shoulders are tense. Tell me what's wrong." He turned to face her head on.

She didn't want to tell him, but she didn't want to hold back either. "I had to talk to Hannah about Hank."

Deacon's eyes narrowed. "Hank?"

"At the meeting Thursday. I didn't want to make a big deal about it. But she's had a thing for him for a while now, and after what he said to me on Thursday…"

"About the rose garden?"

"Partly. He also…" Callie hesitated. She wasn't sure telling Deacon was the right thing to do. "He kind of, sort of, propositioned me."

Deacon drew back, his expression turning to thunder. "He *what*?"

"It wasn't exactly that blatant. He suggested a relationship between the two of us. He seemed to think I would be a political asset, and he could use his power as Mayor to solve problems for me."

Deacon was still. "What did you tell him?"

The question surprised her. "That I wouldn't even consider it."

"In those exact words?"

"Yes." Then she rethought the vehemence of her answer. "I mean at first, yes. That's what I said. But I may have hinted later, a little bit, that I'd think about it. But—"

"*Are* you thinking about it?"

"It was a ruse. I wanted to get out of the conversation."

Deacon leaned in a bit. "Does he believe you're still thinking about it?"

"It doesn't matter. I'm not."

"Don't."

"I won't."

"Good."

"Deacon?"

"Yeah?"

"Are you angry?"

He looked angry. "No."

"That wasn't very convincing."

He wrapped her hand in his and started walking again. “Hank ticks me off.”

“I used to think he was a decent guy.”

“He’s not.”

“I know that now.”

“You shouldn’t—” Deacon raked his free hand through his hair and gave his head a quick shake. “You know what? We’re not going to talk about him anymore. Home to the boys?”

She liked the way that sounded. It was a relief. “Yes. Home to the boys.”

Deacon knew he had to speed up his plan. Hank wasn’t going to go away quietly. He was going to use every bit of leverage to win Callie over. She might not particularly like Hank, but Deacon couldn’t be sure what factors she’d take into account. He couldn’t afford to wait for Hank’s next move.

Though it was too early in their relationship, making it more of a risk than Deacon would like, three days later he headed into a jewelry store.

It was quiet and cool inside. Thick grey carpet cushioned his feet, and he was surrounded by bright turquoise tones and curved glass display cases that sparkled under suspended lights.

“Can I help you, sir?” A crisply dressed and very professional-looking thirtysomething woman approached him.

“I need something fantastic,” he said. He didn’t have a particular style in mind. He only knew he wanted to knock Callie’s socks off when she opened the box.

“In a ring?” the woman asked.

“An engagement ring,” he clarified.

She gave him a warm smile. “You’ve definitely come

to the right place. Were you leaning toward traditional or modern?"

"I was leaning toward fantastic."

Her grin widened. "Did you have a price range in mind?"

"No. If it's the right ring, price doesn't matter."

"Okay." She gestured to a round display case in the middle of the store and moved gracefully to it. "Let me show you what we have here in the 'fantastic' case."

Her joke got him to smile, and he felt himself relax. It was a strange situation to be sure. But there was no reason he couldn't be friendly with the clerk.

"Please do," he said.

She slipped through an opening into the middle of the round display. Then she unlocked a glass door and selected one…and then two…and then three diamond rings.

"These are the most common solitaire shapes," she said. "Round, emerald and marquis. If you're interested in overall brilliance, the round cut is most popular."

"What about quality?" he asked.

She pulled out a fourth ring. "This is a D flawless, excellent cut."

She handed him a magnifier.

He dutifully took it, and he had to admit the diamond looked great. But he didn't think Callie would look that closely.

He handed back the magnifier and set down the ring. "How about this? If I was asking you to marry me, which ring would you want me to buy?"

The sales clerk looked surprised by the question.

"You must have a favorite," he said.

"I have a few favorites. What are you trying to say? Beyond the proposal itself, what are you trying to say to her with the ring?"

"That I'm the best choice, and I'll take care of her and her children forever." The answer popped out before Deacon could think it through.

"Ahh." The woman's eyes danced with delight. "I know just the ring."

She crossed to the opposite side of the display, slid open another case, before returning with a snow-white leather box. It held a ring with a large, round center stone, set within a whimsically swirled and twisted band of platinum and yellow gold, further decorated with tiny diamonds.

"It's our finest stone," she said, her voice almost reverent, as she leaned forward to look with Deacon. "In a timeless but modern setting." She drew back. "I'd marry you if you gave me that."

Deacon chuckled. "Sold."

"Really? Do you want to know the price?"

He drew out his wallet to extract his credit card. "Not particularly."

She laughed as she took the card. "I'd so marry you." As she backed away, she waggled the card in his direction. "If she turns you down, keep me in mind."

Deacon grinned in acknowledgement of her joke, but inside, he was anxious all over again. Callie could turn him down. She could easily turn him down.

The sales clerk rang through the purchase and packaged the ring. She seemed to see something of the uncertainty in his expression.

"It is returnable within sixty days," she told him gently.

"I'll know the answer a whole lot before then."

"Good luck."

"Thanks." He returned his credit card to his wallet and his wallet to his pocket.

On the way out of the store, his phone rang.

A glance at the screen told him it was Tyrell. He didn't want to talk to the man right now.

He had good news. Tyrell would be thrilled to know Deacon was about to propose. But Deacon didn't want to share that information.

He wanted Callie to be the first person to hear.

The ring box tucked in his shirt pocket, he pulled his rental car from the parking space and entered the downtown traffic. Downright Sweet was only ten minutes away, and he'd arranged to meet her for a late lunch.

A fancy candlelight dinner might be a better choice. But he didn't want the audience they'd have in a restaurant. He could ask her at home, after the boys went to sleep. But as much as he found the toy-cluttered living room relaxing and comfortable, it didn't exactly shout romance.

He'd take her to the patio of the View Stop Café. They could take the winding river path from the parking lot. They could step off into the flower garden. Amongst the bright azaleas and the swaying willow trees, he'd pop the question.

He drove to Downright Sweet and saw Callie standing on the sidewalk. She was gorgeous in the sunshine, her hair freshly brushed and taken down from her usual ponytail, a soft white lace-trimmed blouse topping a pair of fitted dark slacks.

She'd changed her shoes. He knew she wore flats in the bakery, but she was wearing a pair of strappy black heeled sandals. They accentuated the length of her toned legs and showed off her pretty feet.

He came to a halt.

Before he could hop out and open the door, she was inside, buckling up.

"Having a good day?" he asked.

"Hank came by."

"What? Why? What did he do?" The last thing Deacon wanted to think about today was Hank.

"I didn't come out of the back. Hannah gave him the cold shoulder. He didn't stick around long."

"He'll be back." Of that, Deacon was sure.

Deacon touched his hand to the bulge in his shirt pocket. He wanted Hank out of the picture for good.

"View Stop Café?" he asked.

"Perfect."

Deacon drove the mile to get them there. Traffic was light that summer afternoon, and the lights seemed to be in his favor. He was breezing through the second green in a row, counting his good fortune, when a white pickup barreled through the intersection, against the red, heading straight for Callie's door.

Deacon spun the wheel to turn her out of the way a split second before the pickup smashed into the back quarter panel, sending them into an uncontrolled spin. His car slammed into a light pole on the passenger side, all but folding in half.

Deacon shook his head to clear his vision as he turned to Callie. "Are you all right?"

She moaned.

"Callie?" He was afraid to touch her.

He released his seatbelt and leaned around to look at her. People were rushing to the windows, shouting at him from outside. He barely heard them.

Callie's eyes were closed, she was slumped sideways and her forehead was bleeding.

Callie had only been stunned for a couple of minutes. She tried to tell the ambulance attendant that she was fine, but he only responded with soothing words, telling her to lie back on the stretcher and relax. Eventually she gave up, closing her eyes while the vehicle swayed beneath her.

She didn't hear sirens. She had to think that was a good sign.

Her head did hurt, but it wasn't unbearable. She reached up to touch the spot, but the attendant gently grasped her hand, stopping her.

"You'll need stitches," he said.

She opened her eyes again. "Really?"

"Only a few. Your hair will hide the scar. Does anything else hurt? Can you wiggle your fingers and toes?"

Callie tested. Everything seemed to work fine. "I think I hit my shoulder."

"You did," he said. "You have a bruise. But it doesn't seem to be broken. They'll x-ray you at the hospital."

"I don't need a hospital." Now that the shock was wearing off, embarrassment was setting in. She was about to arrive at the hospital on a stretcher. It really was overkill.

"Deacon is okay?" She looked for confirmation. "The driver?"

She remembered him talking to her in the car, and then she'd seen him speaking to the police while she was wheeled away. He'd looked okay, but she didn't know for sure.

"I can tell you there was only one ambulance called to the scene."

She assumed that was good.

"Here we are," the paramedic said.

The ambulance slowed and came to a stop.

The back doors opened, and sunlight flooded in.

Callie closed her eyes against the glare. The movement of the stretcher made her dizzy, so she kept them closed.

She could feel the temperature change when they entered the hospital. She heard voices, a nurse directing them and then the swoosh of a privacy curtain closing. The movement stopped, and she opened her eyes.

There was a woman standing over her.

“Hello, Mrs. Clarkson,” she said. “I’m Dr. Westhall. You’ve been in a car accident.”

“I remember,” Callie said.

“Can you tell me what day this is?”

“Wednesday. It’s May 30th.”

“That’s good,” the doctor said, flashing a little light in Callie’s eyes.

“I didn’t lose my memory.”

“I’d be surprised if you had. But you’ve had a good bump, and you’ll need three or four stitches.”

Deacon suddenly appeared beside the doctor, his face pale, his expression grave. “Callie. Are you all right?” He took her hand.

“Are you Mr. Clarkson?” the doctor asked.

A pained expression crossed Deacon’s face. “No. I’m her boyfriend.”

The words surprised Callie. Her boyfriend? Deacon considered himself her boyfriend?

Her chest warmed, and she couldn’t hold back a smile.

He sat down on the opposite side of the bed to the doctor and held Callie’s hand in both of his.

“I’m fine,” she said.

“I’m so sorry.”

“It wasn’t your fault. The guy ran that light.”

The doctor wrapped a blood pressure cuff around Callie’s arm, and it whined as it tightened.

“I should have seen him coming.”

"You turned," she said. She had a sudden memory flash of the truck's heavy duty grill coming straight at her. "If you hadn't turned..." She would have been crushed.

He pressed her hand against his lips.

"I'm going to put in some freezing," the doctor told her as she inspected Callie's forehead.

"Sure."

"I'm thinking I'll go with five stitches. The smaller the scar, the better."

"I'm not worried about a little scar," Callie said.

Deacon's attention went to the cut. "Your hair will probably cover it."

"I'm really not worried." She wasn't sure why everybody seemed so concerned about a little scar on her forehead.

Life happened. People got banged up. Nobody stayed pristine.

"When I'm done, we'll take an X-ray of that shoulder."

The concern came instantly back to Deacon's face. "You hurt your shoulder, too? Anything else?"

"It's just a bruise," Callie told him. She could feel the freezing start to work, and the stinging went away from her forehead.

"I'll feel better when we get an actual medical diagnosis. What else did you hit?"

"Everything else feels normal. Did you call Hannah? Can Pam stay with the boys?" Callie glanced at her watch. She didn't know how long an X-ray would take, but Pam was due to drop the boys off at the bakery at four.

"I've talked to Hannah. And I've talked to Pam. She has plans, but I'll pick up the boys. I can take them home. Unless you want me to bring them here?"

"No." She started to shake her head.

"Hold still," the doctor said.

"Sorry. Don't bring them here. I don't want to scare them." Callie couldn't help but think that the last time her sons were at a hospital, their father had died.

Not that Ethan remembered. But James might.

"I'll arrange for a car to take you home," Deacon said.

"I can call a cab."

"I'll set something up."

His offer warmed her. She felt cared for. It was an odd experience.

From her earliest memory, she'd struggled to take care of her sickly mother. Her older brothers had been lazy louts. At eight years old she'd already been cooking and cleaning for them.

Frederick had been wonderful. But his physical limitations meant she was the caregiver. She was the one who managed the physical necessities of life for herself, the boys and Frederick.

But now Deacon was her boyfriend. That's what boyfriends did. They took care of their girlfriends, and their girlfriend's sons. She couldn't help but smile again.

Deacon was her boyfriend.

Seven

Deacon finished reading a story to James and Ethan. He'd told them their mommy had a headache and was going to bed early. Luckily, they didn't ask any questions. They both seemed content to let Deacon give them a bath—an exciting experience for Deacon—and get them into their pajamas and tucked into bed.

Ethan had fallen asleep during the last pages of *Wilbur the Little Lost Pony*, and James was giving slow blinks, looking cozy under his rocket ship comforter. Deacon quietly closed the book and left their bedroom.

He made his way to the opposite end of the hall, through the open double doors to Callie's room. She was sitting up in bed, with a tablet on her lap and a small white bandage on her forehead. She was wearing a pretty pastel nightie with lace around the shoulders and across the neckline. Her hair was lustrous in the yellow lamplight.

"You're awake," he said softly.

"It's only eight o'clock."

He came forward to sit on the edge of the bed. "Sleep would be good for you."

"I have a boo-boo," she said. "I'm not sick."

"You almost got a concussion." He couldn't help himself, he smoothed her hair back on the uninjured side of her forehead.

"I came nowhere near to getting a concussion." She paused, and her eyes shadowed. "Thanks to you."

"I'm just glad you were okay." He moved closer and drew her gently to him.

She set aside the tablet and hugged him back. She felt perfect in his arms.

"Did the boys fall asleep?" she asked against his shoulder.

"Ethan did. James is almost there. I read them the pony story."

There was a smile in her voice. "They love that one."

"They're amazing kids."

"I'm so lucky to have them." She wiggled against him, then suddenly drew back. "What *is* that?" She pointed to his shirt pocket.

It was the ring box bulging out against her.

The circumstances were hardly ideal. He knew he should wait a couple of days. He knew he should give her a chance to feel better. He knew he should do it somewhere more romantic.

He wanted a yes.

Above everything else, he wanted a yes.

But he suddenly didn't want to wait another second.

He let his emotions rule his judgement and reached into his pocket. He extracted the box and handed it to her.

Looking half perplexed, half intrigued, she flipped it open.

Her expression froze as she stared at the diamond ring.

He knew immediately that he'd made a mistake, and he had to fix it somehow. "I know this might seem sudden. But, Callie, if one thing has become clear to me these past weeks, it's my feelings for you. I'm crazy about you. I'm crazy about your sons. We're good together. We belong together. We can have such an amazing and wonderful life together."

She lifted her gaze to his. "Are you…"

"Marry me, Callie. Make me the happiest man in the world."

"I…" She seemed to stumble over her words. "When… Why… How…"

"Why? Because you're amazing. When? I think the second I saw you. And how, well, a very nice woman at the jewelry store helped me buy this."

"Deacon, this is…" She hadn't said yes, but she hadn't said no either. She was hesitating.

He couldn't tell if she was simply acting the part of a tentative, newly widowed woman, or if she thought another man, someone like Hank, would be better for her.

"I can give you a fantastic life," Deacon said. "Both you and the boys. You'll have everything and anything you need."

Her voice was soft, cautious, nervous. "Do you love me, Deacon?"

He couldn't bring himself to utter the ultimate lie. "I am head over heels," he said instead.

"I love you, too." Clearly, she was a woman who could go all in.

He admired that, even as it put him slightly off balance.

"Is that a yes?" he asked.

"Yes. It's a yes." She wrapped her arms around his neck, and he gathered her close against him.

"Don't let me hurt you," he said, restraining himself, trying to be gentle.

"You're not hurting me."

There was a sheen in her eyes as she drew back, holding out her hand. It trembled ever so slightly.

As he took the ring and slipped it on, a cramp formed in the pit of his stomach.

It was happening. She was going to marry him, and his impossible childhood fantasy was going to come true.

He should have been thrilled.

He should have been over the moon.

But something didn't feel right. No, something felt too right.

Callie was too good at playing her part. She was taking his emotions along on the ride, and there seemed to be nothing he could do to stop it.

"Make love to me, Deacon."

He hesitated, his conflicting emotions trampling all over each other. "I don't want to hurt you," was his excuse.

But she stripped her nightie over her head. "You're not going to hurt me."

She was beautiful. She was beyond beautiful. She was perfect.

There was nothing he wanted more than Callie in his arms. He wanted this to be real. Once again, he asked himself, *where was the harm?* She was getting what she wanted. And he was definitely getting what he wanted.

Why not delve completely into the fantasy?

He kissed her mouth, wider, longer, deeper. He closed a hand over her breast, feeling her nipple bead into his palm. He firmed his forearm across her lower back, easing her down on the mattress, resting her head on the white pillow.

The words *I love you* formed inside his brain. But he didn't dare let himself go that far.

His phone rang in his pocket. He knew deep down it would be Tyrell.

He shut if off without looking, then he stripped off his clothes, pulled back the covers and lay down beside Callie.

She cradled his face with her hands. "The boys adore you."

"I'll do right by them." He promised himself as much as he promised her.

He'd bonded with her sons in a way he hadn't expected. They'd be his responsibility from here on in. As his half nephews, they were his blood relatives on top of everything else. No matter what happened, he'd make sure they were cared for and protected forever.

She kissed him. "I can't believe this is happening."

"Neither can I." That part was the absolute truth.

Callie's life galloped forward at breakneck speed.

The Mobi Transportation project was still just an idea on paper, so Deacon wanted Callie and the boys to move to Hale Harbor. Deacon said it made sense to keep her house in Charleston, because they'd be back and forth quite often.

At first she didn't see how she could up and move out of Charleston. But Hannah eagerly offered to take over management of the bakery. Deacon confessed to having made another donation to the City Beautification Committee to get them to move the rose garden.

At first Callie was stunned and annoyed that he'd gone against her wishes. But then she saw Hannah's reaction, and she knew he'd solved a big problem for them. He'd also circumvented Hank. And, on Hannah's behalf, Callie appreciated that. So she decided to forgive him.

Before long, Callie realized that living in Hale Harbor was a realistic option.

She'd expected they'd have a small wedding, but Deacon was in a hurry for that, too. He wanted to rush down to the courthouse and sign the paperwork. She found the idea sorely lacking in romance.

But Deacon argued that couples were wrong to fixate on the wedding. Personally, he was focused on the marriage, and he wanted to get to the heart of their relationship as quickly as possible.

She had to admit, he actually made the courthouse idea sound romantic. She also had to admit she admired his practicality. She also admired his efficiency. And she found herself anxious to get started on their new life.

So newly married, they'd landed at the small airport in Hale Harbor. Deacon had chartered a plane, explaining that the number of connections they'd need to get in and out of small airports would be hard on the boys.

She hadn't stopped to think about Deacon's wealth before now. She knew he had money, but somehow, she hadn't expected it to be at this level—maybe first-class tickets and maybe five star hotels, but chartering an entire jet? She experienced a new wave of uncertainty at the pace of everything.

But when they arrived at his house, she was relieved. It was nice. It was beautiful. It was even generous in size. But it wasn't a mansion. She'd been worried that he might have a household staff and a dozen luxury cars lined up in air-conditioned garages.

Then when he showed her into the boys' bedroom, her heart nearly burst.

It was larger than their old bedroom, and the windows were in different places, and there was a connected bathroom, but otherwise, it was identical to their room in Charleston.

"I wanted them to feel at home," he told her as the boys hopped onto James's bed.

"How did you do this?" She took a step inside, even James's rocket ship comforter and the train pictures hanging on the wall were the same.

"I took some pictures and sent them to my housekeeper. She's a miracle worker."

"You have a housekeeper?" Callie asked, getting nervous again.

"She comes in a couple of times a week."

James scooted across the blue carpet to his dresser. "Our clothes go here."

"Don't tell me you changed the carpets," Callie said, realizing it was a near match to her house.

Deacon shrugged. "They were getting worn anyway. I wanted to go all in." He raised his voice a little. "If your mom wants to give you a bath, I'll bring up your suitcases and unpack."

"You're too much," she said.

She wanted to ask him exactly how much money he had to throw around on frivolous things, but the question was going to have to wait. It had been a very long day, and the boys were going to get cranky soon. She wanted to have them tucked into bed before exhaustion set in.

By the time she had them bathed and toweled off, Deacon had their clothes unpacked and their pajamas laid out on the bed. Callie couldn't help but appreciate the extra help. It took only minutes for the boys to be happily tucked into bed.

Outside the boys' room was a loft overlooking a

curved staircase, with a spare room next door, facing out the front of the house. Past the staircase, a short hallway led to the master bedroom. It was magnificent, a very large room with a high ceiling, an adjacent sitting room, a huge master bathroom and a giant walk-in closet that was only about a third filled with Deacon's suits and clothing.

"This is gorgeous," Callie said, turning to look from all angles.

"It was one of the things that sold me on this house plan. I like space around me. I don't like feeling cramped."

"When did you buy it?" she asked.

"Three years ago. The company had a good year, and the dividend payment was unusually high. Besides, I'd never intended for my apartment to be permanent."

"Was it new when you bought it?" Callie hadn't seen anything in the house that looked remotely worn.

"I'd bought the building lot a while ago, so it was just a matter of finding the right plan. Do you want to unpack, or look around a bit first?"

"Can I look around?"

"You can do whatever you want."

She made her way back to the staircase, passing another loft that overlooked the two-story living room. At the bottom of the stairs, the foyer opened to a library on one side and a formal dining room on the other. Moving to the back of the house, she came to the two-story living room with an arched bank of windows facing the yard and connected to an open-concept kitchen, breakfast nook and family room.

"There's a covered porch off the family room." Deacon flicked a switch and lit up a generously sized deck with padded all-weather furniture and a hot tub.

"Is the hot tub secure?" The thought of Ethan accidentally falling in made her nervous.

"I put a lock on the cover."

She turned to glance behind her, taking in the sparkling kitchen, the pristine family room furniture, the art work and fixtures.

"I don't know how to ask this," she said, walking back, trailing her fingertips along the burgundy leather sofa.

He followed. "Ask away."

She abruptly faced him. "I didn't think… I mean, we never discussed… How, um, rich are you?"

"On a scale of one to ten?"

"You know what I mean."

His expression became a little guarded. "I have enough to support us."

It was a nonanswer.

From what she'd seen, he had far more than enough to support them.

She tried to put her concerns into words. "It's a little… This wasn't exactly what I was expecting."

He crossed his arms over his chest, his lips pursing as if she'd annoyed him. "You don't waste any time, do you?"

She didn't understand. She struggled with how to phrase it. "I can't help wondering how much my life is going to change."

"I didn't really want to do this tonight," he said.

"This?"

He kept talking. "I hoped we could have a little dignity about it."

"Dignity?"

Was he secretive about his money? If he wanted to keep it private, she supposed she could live with that. But it was an odd way to start a marriage.

"Why don't you go first?" he said.

The question baffled her. "Go first at what?"

"Why did you hide Frederick's money?"

"Hide it where?"

Did he mean by buying the bakery? That wasn't hidden. And hidden from whom?

"I think we're past playing coy, Callie."

"Deacon, if you don't want to talk about your money..."

"I don't want it to be one sided."

She peered at his expression, trying to figure out what was going on. "Okay..."

"Good," he said. "What's your net worth?"

The question confused her even more. He'd seen her house, her business. He knew her lifestyle.

"You mean the house and the bakery?"

Deacon looked impatient. "I mean Frederick's money."

She cast around for an answer. The few thousand dollars in her savings account didn't seem worth talking about.

"Frederick didn't have a life insurance policy," she said. "Not with the injuries to his lungs."

"I meant his family money."

"What family money?"

He threw up his hands. "This is getting us nowhere."

She was feeling as frustrated as he sounded. "Then tell me what you want? What are you talking about?"

"I'm talking about the Clarkson family fortune?"

He was joking. He had to be joking.

She waited for him to laugh, but he didn't.

She braced her hand on the back of the sofa. Something was terribly wrong with this conversation.

Deacon couldn't figure out what Callie had to gain by continuing to pretend. They were married now. The deal was done.

They'd played each other. But they'd both done it. They were both bringing something to the table, and they were both getting what they wanted.

"I know all about Frederick's family," he said. "So let's just figure out how this is going to work."

She still didn't drop the act. "What about Frederick's family?"

"I grew up in Hale Harbor."

She didn't respond. If anything, she looked even more confused.

"Everyone in Hale Harbor knows the Clarksons. The castle, the Port, their history, their *money*."

"Frederick's family lives in Miami."

The statement stopped Deacon cold.

Either she was the greatest actress on the planet, or she believed what she'd just said.

Plus, there was no reason for her to have made that up. There was no benefit to that particular lie. Was there?

"They don't have a fortune," she continued. "They sure don't have a castle."

A feeling of unease crept into Deacon. If Frederick had lied to her, where had his money gone?

Deacon frantically reframed a world where Callie hadn't known about Frederick's money.

Her hold on the sofa tightened. Her expression hardened, and she gestured around the room. "Is this all a sham, Deacon? Are you a con artist? Are you under the impression that, by marrying me, you'll get your hands on a fortune? Are you in debt, is that it?"

"No!"

"You didn't want a prenup. I thought that was odd. I should have listened to myself." She turned to leave the room.

His brain was struggling to make sense of everything. "Callie, something's wrong."

"You bet it is," she called over her shoulder.

"Frederick lied to you."

She gave a slightly hysterical laugh. "It's *you* who lied, Deacon." She kept walking.

He rushed across the living room and caught up to her in the foyer.

"You can divorce me," she said. "And go find yourself some other rich woman to marry."

"I don't want your money."

The front doorbell rang.

"I'll be out of here in the morning," she told him.

"Deacon?" a man's voice called through the door.

Deacon recognized Tyrell's voice and swore under his breath.

Callie started up the stairs.

"I can explain," he called after her.

She didn't answer.

"Deacon," Tyrell called out again.

Deacon was torn between going after her and getting rid of Tyrell. The last thing he needed was Frederick's father in the mix of all this.

He dragged open the door. "*What* are you doing here?"

Before the words were even out, he saw that Margo was with him.

"Where are my grandsons?" she asked, a desperate hunger in her eyes.

"They're asleep," Deacon said.

"But they're here."

"You were supposed to call," Tyrell said.

"And I *will*," Deacon countered.

Margo started forward.

"You have to *leave*," Deacon said, blocking her from entering and glancing behind him.

He was fairly sure Callie wouldn't come back downstairs, but he didn't dare chance it.

"I want to see them," Margo said.

"I told you, they're asleep."

"I won't wake them."

Deacon looked at Tyrell. "Take her home or you'll blow everything."

He could see the hesitation on Tyrell's face.

"Now," Deacon said.

"I've waited so long," Margo wailed.

"Darling." Tyrell put a hand on his wife's arm. "We have to—"

"You can't make me wait," she cried, shaking Tyrell off. "And *him*." She pointed to Deacon. "He's the last person who should stop me from seeing my grandsons." She surged forward.

Deacon planted himself directly in front of her. "You may not like me. You may even hate me. But this is my house, and Callie is my wife, and you are not getting past me to see those boys."

"How *dare* you."

He heard a noise behind him.

"Deacon?" Callie asked.

His stomach turned to lead.

"What's going on?" she asked.

"Is that her?" Margo asked.

"Go," Deacon hissed.

"Grandsons?" Callie asked.

He turned to face her, blocking the opening of the door. "I told you I could explain."

"Who are those people?"

Deacon fought it for several seconds, but then gave in to the inevitable. “They are Frederick’s parents.”

The color drained from Callie’s face.

“They’ve been estranged from Frederick for years,” Deacon quickly explained. “He didn’t tell you about them, because he didn’t speak to them.”

She looked like she might keel over, and he rushed forward to support her. He grasped her shoulder and put an arm around her waist.

“Are you Callie?” Margo asked.

Deacon saw that the door was wide open, and Margo had stepped inside.

“I’m sorry,” he whispered in Callie’s ear. “I’m so sorry.”

“I’m Frederick’s mother,” Margo said.

Tyrell entered, as well. “I’m Tyrell Clarkson. This is my wife, Margo.”

Callie tipped her head to look at Deacon.

“Can we do this tomorrow?” he asked Tyrell.

“I’ve waited so long,” Margo said. “Can I please see my grandsons?”

“They’re asleep.” Callie’s whisper was paper dry.

“I promise I’ll be quiet,” Margo said. Her longing was so painfully obvious, that even Deacon felt sorry for her.

“You don’t have to do this,” Deacon said to Callie. “She has no right to ask.”

Margo glared at Deacon.

“You’re their grandmother?” Callie asked Margo. The bewilderment was clear in her tone.

Margo nodded.

“You knew this?” Callie said to Deacon.

“I was trying to figure out how to tell you. I thought—” Deacon stopped himself. There was no way he was having this conversation in front of Tyrell and Margo. "I'll explain. But not right now."

"I don't have Frederick's money," Callie told Deacon.

"I don't want Frederick's money."

"What happened to Frederick's money?" Tyrell asked.

"Back off," Deacon ordered.

"He gave it to charity," Callie said. "Spinal cord research."

"His entire trust fund?" There was skepticism in Tyrell's tone. "Millions of dollars?"

"He never told me how much. He once said he regretted it. He didn't know he'd have the boys."

"I have no interest in Frederick's money," Deacon said to Callie. To Tyrell, he said, "Can you not see that you should leave."

"But—" There was a tremor in Margo's voice.

"Not tonight," Deacon said.

"You can come up and see them," Callie said.

Deacon looked at her, dumbfounded.

Hope rose in Margo's expression.

"For a quick minute," Callie said. "If we're really quiet."

Margo gave a rapid nod.

Callie disentangled herself from Deacon. "This way."

She started up the stairs, and Margo was quick to follow.

"You better start talking," Callie said to Deacon as she marched into the family room.

She'd sat in the boys' room for an hour after Margo left. Instinct had told her to curl up next to James for the night and try to block out everything she'd just learned. But she knew she'd never sleep. There was no point in putting off the confrontation with Deacon.

"Will you sit?" he asked.

He was in a leather armchair, next to the stone fireplace, a tumbler of amber liquor on the table beside him.

There was nothing to be gained by standing. So she took the opposite chair. The thick cushions cradled her weight.

"Something to drink?" he asked.

"No."

"Okay." He sat forward. "From the beginning. When I first came to Charleston, I already knew who you were."

"What did you want from me?"

"I wanted to meet you. Tyrell was curious about his grandsons. He was also afraid of approaching you. He thought Frederick had turned you against them, so he didn't want to introduce himself."

"Why you?"

Deacon hesitated.

She peered at him. "Are you making up a lie?"

"I'm thinking about how to phrase the truth."

She scoffed at the semantics, wishing now that she'd said yes to a drink.

"It was because I'm only tangentially connected to the family," Deacon said. "Tyrell thought you'd know the rest of them, but not me."

"What does *tangentially* mean?" She hated the way he was talking in riddles.

Deacon was hiding something. He was probably hiding a lot. When she let herself think about what she'd lost here tonight, her stomach curled into a ball, and tears burned behind her eyes.

"I'm Tyrell's illegitimate son."

Callie sat up straight, nearly coming out of her chair. "You're Frederick's *brother*?"

"Half brother. And we never knew each other. I'm not sure he knew I existed."

"But his father did."

"Oh, yes. Tyrell has known about me all along."

Callie sat back, trying frantically to digest the information.

Deacon rose and crossed the room.

When he came back, he handed her a glass.

"Brandy," he said.

She thought about refusing, but it seemed like a better idea to drink it down.

She accepted the glass and took a healthy swallow.

"You don't love me," she noted as he sat down. Of everything that had been revealed, that was the fact that burned most sharply in her mind.

Deacon sat back down and again took his time responding. "I was amazed at how much I liked you."

"Am I supposed to be grateful for that?" She could add mortification to her list of unwelcome emotions. She'd honestly thought she loved him, that she was *in love* with him, that he was the love of her life.

He, on the other hand, had been faking it the whole time.

"I thought you were after my money," he said.

"I wasn't."

"I don't mean that in a bad way."

"There's a good way to accuse me of being a gold digger?" She took another drink.

"You as much as admitted to marrying Frederick for his money. I thought I was the next step on the ladder."

"But you stayed after that. It doesn't make sense that you stayed."

She knew she was tired. She was emotionally drained. This was probably the very worst day of her life, and her brain was foggy. But it was nonsensical that he'd stuck around if he thought she was using him.

"There are a lot of different relationships in the world. I guess I didn't mind that you were pragmatic about bettering your circumstances."

"You thought I was pretending to fall for you?"

What kind of a man was he? She thought back to the time they'd spent together, the fun they'd had, the nights in her house, the beach with the boys. All that time, he'd thought she was playing him?

"I liked you a lot," he said, toying with his glass, turning it in a circle on the wooden coaster. "I didn't know where it was going, and I wanted to find out."

"So you *proposed*? You *married* me to find out where it was going?" She took another healthy swallow of the brandy.

"I knew Watkins was pursuing you, and, well…I couldn't afford to wait."

"I had no interest in Hank." She was revolted by the thought of even kissing Hank. There was no way she would have embarked on a relationship with him.

"I know that now," Deacon said.

She polished off her drink. "I don't know what you thought was going to happen here. But I'm leaving in the morning. I'm filing for divorce. You've messed up my life—"

"I wish you wouldn't do that."

"Too bad."

"I think we can make this work."

She laughed. It sounded a bit hysterical. It probably was.

"Make it work?" she repeated. "In what universe is there anything here to make work?"

"I was wrong. I thought I was giving you what you wanted, another wealthy husband."

"It had nothing to do with wealth." She didn't know why she made the point. She didn't care anything about Deacon's opinion of her. "Frederick begged me to marry him. He knew I wasn't in love with him. But he was kind, and he said I made him happy, and I wanted to be a mother. I didn't want to stay in Gainwall and—"

"You don't have to explain it to me."

"I hate what you thought of me."

"I was wrong. I knew the Clarksons wanted their grandsons. I thought you wanted money. We got along fine. We got along better than fine."

Memories of their lovemaking—the ones she'd been desperately trying to keep at bay—suddenly surfaced. She felt her body heat up from her toes to her cheeks.

"Is that how you see it?" she asked. "You had everybody's best interests at heart?"

"I'm saying I knew what they wanted. I thought I knew what you wanted. And it was easy to talk myself into doing it."

"You got it completely wrong."

"I just admitted that."

It was true. He had. She didn't know what else to say.

"Don't leave right away," he said. "It's always an option. It'll stay an option. But there are a lot of people…"

She waited, wondering how he'd intended to end the sentence.

"More brandy?" he asked instead.

She looked down at the empty glass in her hand. She wasn't leaving in the next five minutes. She still had to make it through tonight. "Why not?"

He rose to pour. "You saw how Margo feels."

Callie couldn't help but think back to Margo's expression when she saw her sleeping grandsons. There had been tears in her eyes. She'd slowly crouched down beside James's bed and just stared at him.

"There's no love lost between me and Tyrell, but he is their grandfather. And they have two uncles, Aaron and Beau." Deacon finished pouring her brandy and turned back. "James and Ethan are the spitting images of their uncles."

"I don't care," she said.

This wasn't about uncles. It was about her and her sons. Her chest tightened again thinking about what this would do to her boys. They adored Deacon.

They were barely recovering from the loss of their father. She'd just ripped them away from their lives in Charleston, and now she was going to ruin their foundation all over again. How had this gone so wrong?

"Family matters," Deacon said as he handed back her glass.

A question rose up in Callie's mind. "What happened with Frederick and his family?"

"Something between Frederick and Tyrell. Beyond that, I don't know."

"I don't believe you."

"All I know is that Frederick went off to college and didn't come back afterward. There were rumors that he'd had a falling out with his father."

"You never asked?"

"Asked Tyrell?"

She nodded.

"Tyrell and I don't talk much."

Callie was struggling to put the pieces together. "But he sent you to Charleston."

"That was an anomaly. I was probably his last choice."

She gazed into her glass, the rich amber glowing in the lamplight. “I am leaving.” She had no other choice.

“I know,” he said softly. “I’m only asking for a few days.”

Her heart actually hurt. “I’m not sure if I—”

“You can have your own room. I’ll stay out of your way. Let the boys meet their grandparents. Just take it slow, methodical, make the best choices for the three of you. It’ll be the right thing in the long run.”

She studied his expression, wondering if he was playing her all over again. “What do you get out of this?”

“I like you, Callie. I adore the boys. We’re…compatible.” The sensual glow in his eyes told her what compatible meant. “We could make it work.”

He wasn’t wrong. They were compatible in every way possible.

But staying with him, knowing all this, accepting what he’d done and how he felt about her? She couldn’t do it. It was more than her heart could take.

“That’s not going to happen,” she said, her voice breaking over the words.

Eight

It was 4 a.m. Deacon was in bed, but he wasn't anywhere near to sleeping.

How had he judged her so wrong? Callie wasn't acting. She's wasn't playing him or Hank or anyone else to work her way up the societal ladder.

Down the hall, Ethan cried out in his sleep.

Deacon was on his feet and halfway across the room before he realized he couldn't go to the boy. Callie would go to him. Deacon no longer had the right.

He sat on the edge of the bed, his gaze going to the glowing red numbers on his bedside clock. It was four eleven.

Her heard Callie's voice, indistinct as she tried to soothe Ethan.

Deacon rose again, moving to his open door, listening while Ethan continued to cry.

He heard James's voice, and realized Ethan had woken him up.

He started down the hall. He didn't care how Callie might be feeling about him. It was clear she needed help.

He walked into the room and went straight to James, who was sitting up in bed. Deacon sat down, and James climbed into his lap. He hugged the boy close and looked to Callie.

"He's burning up," she said in a hoarse voice.

"Does he need a doctor?"

"There was a bottle of acetaminophen drops in one of the suitcases."

"I put them in the medicine cabinet." Deacon rose, carrying James with him into the bathroom.

In the glow of the nightlight, he located the medicine. Behind him, Ethan coughed weakly and cried harder.

"Owie," Ethan whimpered.

"I know, sweetheart," Callie said. "We're getting you some medicine."

Ethan sobbed, coughed and sobbed some more. He sounded wretched, and Deacon's heart went out to the poor little guy. Deacon measured out a dose and brought it to Callie.

"We can call a doctor," he said.

"Let's see if this helps first."

Deacon would rather call a doctor right away, but he knew he had to leave the decision to Callie.

She put the medicine dispenser to Ethan's lips. "You need to swallow this, honey," she crooned.

"Yucky," Ethan cried.

"You can have some juice after."

"No."

"It'll make you feel better."

"No, Mommy, no," Ethan wailed, turning his head.

"Ethan." Callie's voice was firm.

"Daddy," Ethan cried, launching himself to Deacon, catching Callie completely off guard.

Deacon quickly grabbed for him, holding James fast in his other arm, gathering the sobbing Ethan against his chest before he could fall to the floor.

Deacon locked onto the staggered expression in Callie's eyes.

"Let me try," he told her softly. "James, can I put you down on the bed?"

Ethan's sobs turned into an uncontrollable cough.

"Mommy?" James asked, his voice trembling. "Is Ethan going to die?"

Callie's eyes filled with tears. She reached for James, taking him from Deacon to hold him in her arms. "No. No. Sweetheart, Ethan is going to be fine. I promise. We just have to give him some medicine."

Deacon took the medication from Callie and sat down on James's bed, holding Ethan close, the little boy's damp face against Deacon's bare chest.

"Does your throat hurt bad?" Deacon asked in a calm voice.

Ethan gave a miserable nod.

Deacon kissed the top of Ethan's head. "I'm sorry, buddy. Do you want it to go away?"

Ethan nodded again.

Deacon was vaguely aware of Callie and James watching him.

"I think I can help." Deacon smoothed Ethan's soft hair. "Do you like honey?"

"On toast," Ethan rasped.

"Not on toast right now. On a spoon. It'll help. Do you think you could swallow some honey on a spoon?"

Ethan nodded.

Deacon rose, carrying Ethan. "Let's go to the kitchen and find some."

"Owie," Ethan whimpered again, as Deacon walked out of the bedroom.

"You know what will work even better than honey on your owie?" Deacon took the stairs. "The yucky medicine."

"Nooo."

"The trick is, you swallow just a little bit of medicine, and before you can even taste it, you pop the honey in your mouth."

James spoke from Callie's arms behind them. "Can I have honey?"

"Sure," Callie said, sounding dazed.

Deacon turned on a small light in the kitchen. He located a bottle of honey and a spoon.

"What do you say, buddy?" He looked down at Ethan. "A quick squirt of yucky medicine and then a big spoon of honey?"

Ethan looked skeptical, and Deacon was afraid his ploy wouldn't work. If it didn't, he was calling a doctor whether Callie liked it or not. Ethan was burning up. They had to get his fever down.

"'Kay," Ethan said in the quietest of voices.

"That's my boy." Relief rushed through Deacon. He held up the medicine dispenser. "I know you can do it, buddy."

Ethan gave a brave nod.

Deacon squirted the medicine into Ethan's mouth.

Ethan screwed up his face in a scowl, but he managed to swallow it.

Deacon quickly put the honey to his lips, and Ethan sucked the spoon into his mouth. His expression slowly cleared.

"That was fantastic," Deacon praised him, wrapping his arms fully around Ethan's sweaty little body.

Callie slumped against the counter, James still in her arms, a single tear escaping to run down her cheek. He held her gaze, and she gave him a shaky nod of thanks.

"Do you want to go back to Mommy?" Deacon asked Ethan.

"'Kay," Ethan squeaked out.

Callie set James down, and Deacon handed her the limp Ethan.

Then Deacon crouched to talk to James. "Honey for you too?"

"Is Ethan okay?" James asked.

"He's going to feel better really soon," Deacon said. "After your honey, you'll need to brush your teeth again."

"Okay," James agreed.

Deacon got a fresh spoon and gave James a small dollop of honey.

He grinned as he licked it.

Callie was sitting at the breakfast table, rocking Ethan in her arms.

Deacon took James's hand. "Back to bed for you."

"Okay," James said, with a last look at his brother.

Deacon helped James with his teeth, got him tucked back in and then returned to the kitchen. Callie was still at the table, rocking Ethan.

Ethan had stopped crying. But his eyes were open, and he cringed in pain as he swallowed.

Deacon crouched beside them.

"Thank you," Callie said, her voice breaking.

"No problem." Deacon was incredibly glad to have been here to support her. "We can still call a doctor."

Callie glanced at her watch. "Let's give the acetaminophen time to work."

"Do you want to move to the family room?" He rose and held out a hand to help her up. "It'll be more comfortable."

She hesitated, but then accepted his offer.

Deacon resisted the urge to put his arm around her. Intellectually, he knew their relationship had irrevocably changed. But emotionally, he still felt protective of her. He still felt close to her. He still felt like her husband.

She sat down in the same armchair as earlier, leaning back with Ethan stretched across her chest.

"Do you want a blanket?" Deacon asked her.

"He called you daddy."

"Yeah." Deacon's chest tightened with the memory. It had taken him completely off guard.

Callie looked wretchedly unhappy, her voice half whisper, half wail. "What am I going to do?"

After Ethan recovered, circumstances seemed to conspire against Callie.

The boys were very obviously bonding with Deacon, and Hannah called full of excitement and ideas as she ran the bakery solo. Margo had had a playroom specially built, and couldn't wait to show it off to her grandsons.

So on Saturday, with Ethan back at full strength, Deacon pulled the car up to the front of the castle.

Callie couldn't do anything but stare in awe at the imposing stone structure. "It looks like a hotel."

"This is where Frederick grew up."

"Daddy used to live here?" James asked in wonder from the back seat.

"He did," Deacon confirmed.

"Was Daddy a prince?"

"He was just a very lucky little boy." There was something in Deacon's voice, but Callie couldn't pinpoint the emotion.

"I wish I was a prince," James said.

Callie had to fight a smile. It was the first time she'd seen humor in the world since she'd discovered the truth.

"When I was a boy, I wanted to be a prince, too," Deacon said.

"There's a tower," James said, excitement growing in his voice. "A real tower. Can I have a sword?"

A part of Callie couldn't help being interested in Frederick's childhood home. But mostly she was plotting their exit from Hale Harbor. The sooner she moved the boys back to their old life, the better it would be for them.

While she helped Ethan out of his car seat, Deacon opened the opposite door for James.

The castle's grounds were vast. Summer flowers were blooming in dozens of garden beds. The lawn was a smooth emerald carpet. Oak trees lined the wide, exposed aggregate driveway. And two lion statues flanked a wide staircase that led to arched oversize wood-plank doors.

The castle was three stories high, with a tower on each of the front corners. She could see at least three gardeners on the grounds. While off to the left side, there was a six-car garage.

"This is ridiculous," she muttered under her breath.

"Down," Ethan said, kicking his legs.

Callie set him down.

He immediately ran for the lawn.

"Don't touch the flowers," she called after him.

James trotted after his brother, while Ethan dropped and rolled in the lush grass.

The door to the castle yawned open. Callie half expected a butler to emerge. But it was Margo and Tyrell who appeared. With them was a young woman who looked to be in her early twenties.

"Who's that?" Callie asked Deacon, dividing her attention between the porch and the boys.

Ethan had spotted a row of rhododendron bushes, and she could almost see his little mind working.

"I don't know. It's not Aaron's wife."

"Another long-lost relative?"

"Not that I know about."

The trio started toward them.

Although it was a warm Saturday, Tyrell was dressed in a business suit. Margo wore tan slacks and a sleeveless patterned silk top. Her grey hair was wispy around her face, while a pair of designer sunglasses were perched on her nose. The other woman was dressed in jeans, a white capped-sleeve T-shirt and flat sandals. She had long blond hair in a sporty ponytail.

"James," Callie called out. "Can you bring Ethan back?"

James trotted over to his brother and took his hand. Ethan pointed at the pink rhododendrons, but James tugged him along.

"I just can't get over it," Margo said as she watched the boys come toward them.

"The genes are strong," Tyrell said.

Callie had learned from Deacon that James and Ethan bore an uncanny resemblance to their uncles, Aaron and Beau.

"I'll have to show you some pictures," Margo said to Callie.

Although she greeted Callie with a squeeze on the arm, Margo didn't acknowledge Deacon.

It was growing clear to Callie that Margo didn't like Deacon. It didn't take a genius to figure out why. It wasn't

Deacon's fault that Tyrell had an affair with his mother. But it seemed as though Margo was determined to hold Deacon responsible.

"Callie, this is Dee Anderson," Margo said. "Dee has a degree in early childhood education, and she's joined our household staff."

Callie let the phrase "joined our household staff" roll around in her brain for a moment.

"Hello, Mrs. Holt." Dee offered her hand.

The name jolted Callie, and she stumbled in her response. "Please, call me Callie." She studiously avoided looking Deacon's way.

Deacon had spent a lot of time at work the past few days. In the evenings, he'd been a big help with the boys. But they'd tiptoed around each other when they were alone. She hadn't talked to him about her immediate plans to stay or go, and he hadn't brought it up.

"Grandma has something special to show you," Margo said to James and Ethan.

James hung back, but she captured Ethan's attention.

"Candy?" asked Ethan.

"It's not candy," Margo said with an indulgent smile.

Ethan frowned.

Callie moved to take each of her sons' hands, putting a cheerful note into her voice. "Why don't we see what Grandma wants to show us?"

James hung on, while Ethan tried to pull out of her hold.

"Do you want some help?" Deacon asked Callie.

"We'll be fine." Margo waved him away and started walking.

"My name is Dee." Dee introduced herself to the boys as she fell into step. "You must be James, and you must be Ethan."

"Ethan," Ethan said.

"It's nice to meet you, Ethan."

"Have candy?"

"Ethan," Callie warned. "You've only just finished breakfast."

"Dessert," Ethan said with authority.

"You know we don't have dessert with breakfast."

"Do you like slides?" Dee asked.

James spoke up. "I like towers." He craned his neck as they walked toward the castle.

Instead of heading for the front door, they took a walkway along the south side of the castle, coming to a chain-link gate that led to a fenced area with a giant, colorful playset of swings, slides, bridges and ladders with safety rails.

James's eyes went wide.

"Slides!" Ethan squealed.

Dee opened the gate, and both boys dashed inside.

"It's…" Callie didn't even know what to say.

"It's consumer tested and very highly rated," Margo said.

"The best safety rating," Dee said.

"I was going to say enormous." Callie stared at straight slides, covered slides, curving slides.

Ethan started up a ladder.

Callie checked his path, looking for the danger zones, deciding where best to stand to spot him. But she didn't see any flaws in the design. There were no spaces where it looked like he could fall. And Dee was right behind him, laughing and asking him what he wanted to try first.

"They seem to like it," Margo said.

"I don't know any kids who wouldn't." Callie looked a little further around. The area was completely fenced. The boys couldn't wander away.

"Would you like to sit down?" Margo gestured to an umbrella-covered table. "I'll have some iced tea brought out for us."

Callie got the feeling she'd been separated from Deacon for a reason. But the boys were happy. Margo was being very hospitable, and Callie preferred to keep her distance from Deacon anyway.

It didn't matter where he was, or what he was doing. She wasn't even going to think about him.

As Deacon signed the paperwork at the boardroom table in the castle's business wing, Beau burst through the door.

"You can't *do* this," Beau shouted at his father.

Tyrell glared at his son for a beat before answering. "Hello, Beau."

"Aaron just told me what's going on."

Tyrell's tone was clipped and even. "Had you not missed the last three board meetings, you might have known sooner."

Beau stalked across the room, making a beeline for the paperwork in front of Deacon.

When Beau reached out to grab it, Deacon jumped from his chair, grabbing Beau's lapel and pushing him back into the wall.

Beau doubled up his fist, and Deacon braced himself for a hit.

"Stop!" Tyrell bellowed.

Beau glared into Deacon's eyes.

"You need a two-thirds majority," Beau spat.

Deacon narrowed his eyes, trying to gauge if Beau was bluffing.

"No," Tyrell said, staying in his seat at the head of the

long table. "You need a two-thirds majority to overturn the decision."

Beau broke eye contact with Deacon to look at his father.

Deacon took a chance and relaxed his hold.

Beau pushed to break free. "Are we going to let the lawyers duke it out?"

Aaron appeared in the doorway, and Deacon felt distinctly outnumbered.

"Do you have the authority to make this deal?" Deacon asked Tyrell.

"Yes," Tyrell said, his voice definitive.

"I will fight you," Beau said. "You are not having this..." He rounded on Deacon. "This *person* replace Frederick."

"He's not replacing Frederick," Tyrell said.

"No?" Aaron walked in and took the chair to the right of his father. Aaron's tone was far more reasonable. "You're giving him Frederick's company shares. He married Frederick's wife. He's here. What more is there to replacing Frederick?"

"We should throw him out," Beau said.

"Beau," Tyrell snapped.

"You're not helping," Aaron said to his brother.

"You're welcome to try," Deacon said easily.

"I'll tie you up in court so long, you'll be bankrupt or retired before we're done."

Deacon sat back down and signed the final paper with a flourish. "Do that, and you'll never see my sons again."

Deacon knew full well Callie could walk away at any moment, and he'd be the one who'd never see James and Ethan again. But for the moment, they were his best leverage point with the Clarksons.

"The price is too high," Beau said to his father. "Even *you* have to know it's way too high."

"They're my grandsons," Tyrell said. "They're the future of this family."

Beau walked around the table and dropped into a chair. "I'll get married," he said. "You win. I'll get married and give you legitimate grandchildren."

"You had your chance," Tyrell said.

Deacon couldn't help but glance at Aaron. Aaron was married. Was there some reason he wasn't having children? From the tight expression on Aaron's face, Deacon guessed that must be the case.

The reason for Tyrell's offer to Deacon was becoming clearer. James and Ethan weren't just his first grandsons. They might well be his only grandsons.

"What's your beef with me?" Deacon asked Beau.

Beau shot a sneer across the table. "Are you kidding me? The mere sight of you is a knife in my mother's heart."

"Not my fault," Deacon said.

"Shouldn't we be talking about his credentials," Aaron asked. "What does he know about running the port? We don't need a useless drain on the system with twenty-five percent voting power."

Deacon was getting tired of this argument. He looked to Tyrell. "Do we have a deal, or don't we? Because I'm the legal guardian of those two boys, and their mother is madly in love with me." The last part was a gross exaggeration at this point, but Deacon liked the way it added to his threat.

Tyrell stood. "There's something you need to see."

At first, Deacon thought Tyrell was talking to him. But it was clear he meant Aaron and Beau.

"What?" Beau asked.

"You can't run this place by decree," Aaron said.

"Will you follow me?" Tyrell's exasperation was clear.

Both men reluctantly followed their father out of the room.

Curious, Deacon went along. Whatever it was Tyrell had up his sleeve, Deacon could only hope it settled the deal.

They made their way along a hallway, through a formal dining room, to a set of glass doors. The doors led to a patio. And when they walked outside, Deacon could hear James's and Ethan's shouts. He also heard a woman's laughter. He guessed it was Dee.

The play area was off the edge of the patio, and both Aaron and Beau moved closer to look. They stopped at the concrete rail, and Deacon watched their expressions as they stared: Aaron at James and Beau at Ethan. It was clear they saw what everyone else did. It was as if they'd been cloned.

Aaron spoke first. "How could that..."

Beau brought the heels of his palms down on the rail, a note of awe in his voice. "Do you think Frederick could see it?"

Tyrell's bet seemed to have paid off. It looked like Aaron and Beau would close ranks around their nephews.

Deacon caught a glimpse of Callie. She was laughing, looking relaxed while she chatted with Margo. She looked unexpectedly happy, and he was jealous. He saw her every day, but he missed her desperately.

His fingertips itched from wanting to touch her. He was longing to hold her. Every time she smiled at her sons, he wanted to kiss her. And at night, he lay awake in a near-constant state of frustration.

She was only steps down the hall in the guest room. He pictured her silk nightgown, her creamy shoulders.

In his mind he saw her sleeping, eyes closed, cheeks flushed, lips slightly parted. He'd kissed her awake more than once. And then…

He gritted his teeth and gave himself a shake, focusing his attention on reality.

As he did, and as he surveyed the scene, a cold realization came over him. It was the boys they wanted. It was Callie they needed. If Callie walked away from him, the Clarksons would welcome her with open arms.

Deacon was entirely expendable.

Callie had let ten days go by.

First Ethan had been sick. Then Margo wanted some time with her grandchildren. She'd asked to take them shopping and to the funfair at the pier. Dee always came along and lent a hand, making Callie feel quite spoiled.

Deacon had stayed busy, working all day, coming home late, making it easy for her to push their problems to the background. He never asked if she was staying, never asked if she was going.

She wanted to leave. But leaving meant telling the world she'd made a mistake, telling Hannah and everyone back in Charleston she'd been a fool. Telling Margo she was taking the boys away. It meant giving a final decision to Deacon and maybe fighting with him about it.

She didn't want to fight with Deacon. She wanted to laugh with him again, talk to him about anything and nothing. She wanted to hold him, kiss him, make love with him and sleep in his arms again. Her soul ached with missing him.

She walked back out onto the deck, in the cool dark of the evening. She'd played with the boys in the hot tub before bundling them off to bed. Now, she picked up the discarded towels and reached in for the floating toys.

Her hand skimmed the warm water. She'd pulled on her cover-up, but her bathing suit was still damp underneath. She was chilled now, and the hot water felt wonderful.

She knew that just inside the door was the wet bar, with wine and brandy, and anything else that might strike her fancy. The moon was full, the lights in the garden glowing, with a view overlooking the town and the dark ocean beyond.

She hadn't spent much time, really no time at all appreciating her surroundings. Deacon had a wonderful house, in a beautiful spot, with every amenity a person could wish for.

Making up her mind, she padded inside, the carpet soft against her bare feet. She found a small snifter, chose a pretty brandy label and poured herself a drink.

She dimmed the lights, discarded her cover-up and lowered herself into the hot water, turning the jets to high and facing the view. She sipped the brandy as the water pulsated against her lower back and surged between her shoulder blades.

"You look comfortable," Deacon said from behind her, his voice deep and melodious.

For a moment, she let the sound wash over her, leaving her skin tingling.

"I didn't know you were here," she said, craning her neck to look at him.

He moved into her view. "I just got home."

"Working late?" A part of her wanted to laugh at the banal conversation, as if they were a normal couple, on a normal night, in a normal circumstance.

He crouched on his haunches and trailed his hand through the water.

She watched with rapt attention, imagining it on her skin.

"Growing pains," he said.

"Hmm?" She forced herself to look up.

"The port is growing, and there are some tough decisions to make."

She was surprised he was sharing. He didn't seem to ever talk about work. She knew he'd lied about Mobi Transportation looking at relocating to Charleston. It was a minor lie in the scheme of things.

It was true that he was a shareholder at Mobi, but his real job was in the family firm of Hale Harbor Port. That was where he worked, with his half brothers, Beau, who seemed hostile, and Aaron, who seemed cold to everyone, not to mention his father, who had, despite Margo's resentment of Deacon, apparently brought him into the family business anyway.

"Mind if I join you?" Deacon asked.

Her heart skipped a beat.

He took in her expression. "I won't if it makes you uncomfortable."

"No. It's fine. It's your hot tub."

He looked like he wanted to say something, but he clamped his lips together.

"Please," she said, gesturing to the water. "It's nice."

He rose. "I'll grab a suit."

She watched him walk away, wishing she could tell him to forget the bathing suit. She'd seen him naked dozens of times. And he'd seen her. And it was silly for them to feign modesty now.

She lowered herself deeper into the water and sipped the brandy, while her mind went on a flight of fancy about making love with Deacon.

He was back before she expected, startling her.

She sat back up, while he climbed into the hot tub with his own glass of brandy. He also set the bottle at the edge.

"Margo mentioned a ball today," Callie said, latching onto a neutral topic.

"The Summer Solstice?" he asked.

"That sounds right."

"It's famous around here, the social event of the year. Everyone wants to be invited to the castle to dance in the grand ballroom."

"The Clarksons apparently have a tailor. She wants to make matching suits for the boys."

Deacon blinked at her. He didn't have to ask the question. They both knew what it was.

The ball was a week away. Would James and Ethan be here to wear their custom-made suits?

"I don't know," Callie told him honestly. "I don't know what to do."

Deacon might be the source of her problem, but he was also the only person who knew the truth. Everyone else thought their marriage was real.

"You know what I want." His tone was deep, sincere, like the words had been pulled from his very core.

She couldn't take her gaze from him. She couldn't speak. She couldn't move.

When he shifted to the seat next to her, her pulse jumped. The water temperature seemed to inch up several degrees.

"Stay," he said. "For as long as you want. I'll give you space." Even as he made the promise, he seemed to grow closer. His gaze moved to her lips. "I'll give you—"

And then he was kissing her. And it was magic. It took her breath away. And she kissed him back, the water sloshing between them. His arms went around her. Her body slid against his. Her breasts plastered again his chest.

A crash shattered the night around them.

They jumped apart, and she realized she'd dropped her brandy snifter on the concrete deck.

"I'm sorry." She couldn't believe she'd been so careless.

She rose to her knees to look over the edge.

"Don't move," he told her, setting his own glass down.

"I'm so stupid," she said.

"I'll clean it up."

"You have bare feet."

"I'll get some shoes."

He turned back to her, wrapping his hands around her shoulders, gazing into her eyes. "I will give you space," he promised.

"That was my fault, too." She had to make the admission.

"What do you want?" he asked. "Just tell me what it is, and I'll do it."

What she wanted was impossible. She wanted the fantasy that had never been true. She wanted their marriage to be what he'd pretended.

"I don't think you can," she whispered.

"Okay," he gave a nod of acceptance. "Okay. But that doesn't mean I won't stop trying."

She watched him rise from the water, the droplets sliding off his broad shoulders, the arms that held her so tightly, his abs, his thighs, everything she'd kissed and touched as they'd made love so many times.

How could he try? What could he possibly do?

There was no way to go back and turn his lies into the truth.

Nine

Deacon dug in and worked hard to learn about Hale Harbor Port. Callie didn't know that his interest in the company was tied to her. She assumed he'd been working there for years, and he hadn't corrected her. So he was on eggshells, thinking she might ask a question he couldn't answer.

Aaron and Beau sure hadn't made the learning curve easy. They wouldn't answer a single question, and Deacon was convinced they were actively turning staff members against him.

But he'd persisted. He'd poured over their billing, accounts payable and receivable, their terminal schedules, traffic volume, even cargo manifests. After hours and hours of work, he'd come to a simple but startling conclusion. Hale Harbor Port was losing money.

He presented his findings to Tyrell, Aaron and Beau at the boardroom table in the castle's business wing.

Tyrell showed little reaction. "We're aware of it," he said.

"It can't continue." Deacon didn't have to fully understand the port business to know that much.

"It's won't continue," Beau said. "It's a temporary slump."

"You have to revise your pricing structure." Deacon didn't buy that it was a temporary slump. He knew from his work at Mobi that the transportation sector had fundamentally changed over the past decade. Everyone had to look at new approaches.

"And price ourselves out of the market?" Beau asked. "It's competitive out there."

"That's obviously not what I meant," Deacon countered.

"What do you mean?" Aaron asked.

Beau turned on his brother. "You're going to take him seriously? He's been here all of five minutes, and you're ready to take his advice."

"Nobody's taking his advice," Tyrell said.

Deacon rocked back in his chair. "Sure. Ignore me. Stick your head in the sand and—" As he spoke, he caught a glimpse of movement through the boardroom window.

He could see all the way across the courtyard, through a window into another part of the castle. It looked like… It was. Callie was in the next wing. He leaned forward for a better view.

"We should at least monitor it," Aaron said.

"We are monitoring it," Tyrell said.

Then Deacon spotted James. He looked disproportionately tall, and Deacon realized he was standing on something. He raised his arms, holding them out to his sides.

"We do have accountants," Beau drawled.

A man approached James, reaching across his outstretched arms. Deacon all but cheered. The man was the tailor. The boys were being measured for suits. They were staying for the ball. Callie was staying for the ball.

A wave of relief passed through Deacon.

"Is that funny?" Tyrell asked.

Deacon refocused his attention. "What?"

"Is it funny that we have accountants?"

"Of course not." Deacon stole one more glance across the courtyard.

James and Ethan were going to look terrific in little tuxedos. Deacon was buying one for himself. He didn't think a tuxedo would come anywhere near to changing Callie's mind about him. But it couldn't hurt either.

"We're not making a major decision today," Tyrell said.

"I'm only suggesting we gather more data," Deacon said, refocusing. "We should look at options."

"What kind of options?" Aaron asked.

"Will you stop humoring him," Beau demanded.

"Vertical integration," Deacon said.

Beau threw up his hands in frustration, but Aaron looked interested.

"Again," Beau said. "He's been here five minutes."

"I've been alive longer than that," Deacon said evenly. "I've been in the transportation industry for years. There's money there. Global supply chains are growing, trade agreements are popping up all over the world. At the retail level, bricks and motor are out, delivery is in. Hale Harbor could be at the nexus of a game-changer."

"Vertical integration." Aaron's head tilted thoughtfully.

"We've operated steady as she goes for hundreds of years," Tyrell said.

"Exclusive agreements," Deacon said to Aaron. "With a firm like Mobi Transport."

"There it is," said Beau. "He wants to use Hale Harbor Port to beef up Mobi."

"It was only an example," Deacon said. "And I meant the other way around, use a company like Mobi Transportation to beef up Hale Harbor Port."

"How?" Aaron asked.

"I've had enough of this." Beau came to his feet.

"We have other business on the agenda," Tyrell said. "But let's break for lunch." He also came to his feet.

Deacon allowed himself another glance across the courtyard, seeing Callie in profile. She was talking to Margo, and the two were watching the tailor try to wrangle Ethan.

Beau and Tyrell left the room, but Aaron stayed seated. He tapped a pen on his leather folder. "How?" he repeated to Deacon.

"Does it matter?" Deacon asked. He knew Aaron was as hostile toward him as Beau. Aaron simply hid it better. "Do you have a good idea or not?"

Deacon figured he had nothing to lose. "Buy or take an equity position in Mobi, or in another company along the chain, like a maritime shipping company. Mobi is nice because it's local, it's small. So a good place to start and test the methodology. Give them preferential pricing, so they use Hale Harbor exclusively."

"*Lower* prices? Lose more money?"

"Increase volume, streamline processes, make the port itself revenue neutral, then get profitable through the subsidiary businesses."

"Do you have *any* idea what you're talking about?"

"I'm only saying it's worth exploring."

"The magnitude of that change is ridiculous."

"You got a better idea?"

Aaron came to his feet. "Not yet. But there has to be a dozen better ideas than that. Beau's right. You've been here five minutes."

Squelching his disappointment, Deacon let his gaze rest on Callie. He might have lost this round with Tyrell and the boys, but Callie was staying, at least for another week. It was a win for him on that front.

"The slump could be temporary," Aaron said.

"Maybe." Deacon didn't think so.

Aaron started for the door. "It always has been in the past."

"This isn't the past," Deacon tossed over his shoulder.

Given the choice between lunch and seeing Callie, he was taking Callie.

He left the boardroom and made his way along the second-floor hallway. The castle was big and rambling, with circuitous hallways, dead ends, multistory grand halls and winding stairways. He had to go up to the third floor and make his way along an open loft hallway, then come down to traverse a kitchen, drawing curious looks from a couple of staff members.

But he finally made it to the other side of the courtyard. He found the second floor and heard the boys' voices.

They were in a dressing room of some kind, though it was the size of a dance hall. He wondered if Margo had all her clothes custom made and if Tyrell and their sons did, as well.

"Daddy," Ethan cried, jumping down from the stool to the obvious chagrin of the tailor.

"What's going on here?" Deacon asked cheerfully as Ethan trotted toward him.

"We're getting new clothes," James answered, heading for Deacon.

"Special, special clothes," Ethan spun around.

Deacon caught Callie's gaze. "You're going to the ball."

Ethan made a throwing motion with his hand.

"There will be dessert," James said.

"You know I like dessert," Deacon said, ruffling Ethan's hair.

Margo kept her attention on the tailor, doing her best to pretend Deacon wasn't there. He wondered how long she planned to keep giving him the cold shoulder. He wasn't going away.

He crossed the room to Callie. "You made a decision?" he asked her on an undertone.

"Time for lunch," Margo said brightly to the boys. "Who wants grilled cheese?"

"Me, me," Ethan said.

"Yes, please," James said.

"Let's go find Dee." Margo hustled the boys out, while the tailor retreated to a table at the far end of the room.

"I should go," Callie said, watching the doorway where her sons had left.

"I'm glad you're staying," Deacon said.

"Don't make any assumptions."

"I'm not."

"It's not for you."

"I know." He wished it was, but he acknowledged full well it wasn't.

"Margo is… She's really grown attached to the boys."

Deacon hadn't seen himself ever being grateful to Margo. But he was now. In this moment, he silently thanked her for her doting ways. It bought him some time.

He didn't know what he was going to do with that time. He had absolutely no plan. But it was better than the alternative.

As she tucked the boys into bed, Callie hoped she was doing the right thing by staying for the ball. It was a form of torture being around Deacon, wanting him, missing him, trying desperately to stay angry with him.

"Mommy," James said as she smoothed the covers around him.

"Yes, sweetheart?"

"Is Grandma very smart?"

"I think so. She seems pretty smart."

"Okay."

"Why do you ask?"

"She says a red tie will make me shine."

"I bet you'll look terrific in a red tie."

"Ethan's snoring again."

Callie listened for a moment. "Just a little bit. It's a quiet snore."

"It sounds like an angry dog."

She gave James a hug. "Your brother's not an angry dog."

"Okay. You're smarter than Grandma."

"I'm glad you think I'm smart." Callie came to her feet. She couldn't help but be warmed by the compliment. She also couldn't help but be curious about the scale James was using to make his assessment.

"Grandma gets mixed up," James said.

"About what?"

"She calls Ethan Beau."

Callie stilled, unnerved, but not completely sure why. "Ethan looks like Uncle Beau did when he was little."

"Uncle Beau looks like an angry dog. He frowns all the time."

"Does Uncle Beau frighten you?"

"No." James sounded completely unconcerned. "I bet he snores."

Callie breathed a sigh of relief. "Good night, James."

"Good night, Mommy."

She left the door partway open as she walked into the hall.

She'd heard Deacon come in while she was reading the boys a story. He was home earlier than usual. She toyed with the idea of going straight to bed. It would be better if she didn't see him tonight. It was emotionally safer to keep her distance.

But she'd left some dishes in the sink, her book was on the table in the family room and she'd been looking forward to a cup of tea. She might struggle with her feelings around him, but she didn't want to hide in her room either.

She started down the stairs.

Deacon was talking, she assumed on the phone. But then she heard another voice. It was oddly familiar, but she couldn't place it.

She followed the sounds into the living room to find the two men standing, facing each other.

Deacon saw her.

The man turned. He was shorter than Deacon, stockier, his hair was long, straggly, and he wore a pair of wrinkled jeans, scuffed black boots and a navy blue T-shirt. The skin of his face looked soft. He had a stubble beard and familiar blue eyes.

"Hello, Callie." His voice sent a shiver down her spine, and she flinched as she recognized him.

"Trevor?" It was her oldest brother, but he sounded frighteningly like her father.

"Long time, no see, baby sister."

"*What* are you doing here?" She hadn't seen or heard from him since the day he stormed out of their tacky little house in Grainwall.

He'd been eighteen. She'd been only nine.

"Is that any way to greet your brother?" He moved toward her.

She was too stunned to move, and he gave her a hug.

She was suddenly transported back to her childhood, to the screaming matches between her brothers and father, to the barked orders for her to bring them beer, make them sandwiches and *to clean that kitchen the hell up*. Everything inside her cringed.

After what seemed like an eternity, he stepped back. "I hear you got married."

She struggled to find her voice. "How did you find me?"

Why had he looked?

After her father had died, one by one, her three brothers had left home, until she was alone with her mother. None of them had ever come back. None of them had helped, not when her mother got sick, not when her mother had died. None of them ever cared that Callie had been orphaned at sixteen.

"Social media. It's a wonderful thing."

"Can I offer you a drink?" Deacon asked. "Please, sit down."

Callie wanted to shout *no*. If Trevor started drinking, he'd never stop.

"Don't mind if I do." Trevor popped himself down on a sofa and patted the seat next to him.

She took an armchair.

"What would you like?" Deacon asked.

"A brew if you've got one." Trevor glanced around the room.

"Merlot, Callie?" Deacon asked, knowing it was one of her favorites.

"I was going to make tea."

"Sure." Deacon left for the kitchen.

"Done real well for yourself, Callie," Trevor drawled.

Now that Deacon was out of the room, Trevor's eyes hardened in appraisal.

Callie's stomach started to hurt. The sights and sounds and smells of her childhood swelled up inside her head. She hadn't thought about her father in years, or her brothers, or even her mother for that matter. But now she pictured her father yelling, her mother sobbing in the corner and Trevor laughing drunkenly.

She couldn't remember who hit whom. There were frequent fistfights amongst the boys, and her dad was quick to slap her mother. Callie herself hadn't been a target. They yelled at her and shoved her, but she didn't remember getting hit.

She did remember being terrified.

"Cat got your tongue?" Trevor asked.

She swallowed. She wanted to tell him to leave, to go away, to never come back. But she couldn't bring herself to do it. The frightened little girl inside her didn't have the courage to stand up.

"Never mind." Trevor looked her up and down. "You don't have to say anything for me to get how it is. You've landed on your feet. I've got my trouble, but you landed on your feet."

Deacon came back, and Callie was incredibly grateful to see him. He carried a mug of tea in one hand and two bottles of beer in the other. He set her tea down beside her, then handed Trevor a beer.

"Are you visiting Hale Harbor?" Deacon asked Trevor. Deacon chose the armchair opposite Callie and twisted the cap off his beer.

"Came to look in on Callie," Trevor said. "Been kicking around Alabama for a while now." He guzzled half his beer.

"Oh. What is it you do?"

"Little of this, little of that."

Deacon glanced at Callie.

She was frozen. She couldn't speak, and she couldn't move. A part of her knew it was ridiculous to be afraid of Trevor. He couldn't do anything, especially not with Deacon here. But she couldn't shake the visceral fear.

Deacon guzzled a good measure of his beer, and Trevor grinned at him in a way that said he'd met a kindred spirit.

"You married my sister," Trevor said.

"I did."

"Didn't get a wedding invitation."

"It was a small wedding."

"Really." Trevor seemed surprised. "I thought you well-to-do people put on posh parties."

"Sometimes," Deacon said politely.

Callie ordered herself to speak up, to say something. It wasn't fair to force Deacon to carry on this conversation with her brother.

Trevor took another long guzzle of his beer.

Callie asked, "Are you married?"

Trevor swung his gaze to her. "Never met the right gal."

Callie was silently grateful on behalf of womenkind. If Trevor had turned out anything like her father—which it seemed he had—then no woman deserved to end up with him.

"No kids either," Trevor said.

Callie did *not* want to talk about her sons. "Have you heard from Joe or Manny?"

She lifted her mug of tea, willing her hand not to shake.

"Can't say that I have. But maybe we should look them up. Maybe we should have ourselves a family reunion."

Callie immediately regretted asking the question.

Deacon polished off his beer and pointedly set down the bottle. "It was nice of you to drop by," he said to Trevor and came to his feet. He glanced at his watch. "Why don't you leave your number, and we'll be in touch."

Trevor looked flummoxed and then annoyed. "Well…" He looked to Callie, but she focused on her tea. "I was…" He didn't seem to know how to counter Deacon's dismissal.

Callie was immensely grateful.

"Sure," Trevor said, polishing off his beer.

He set the bottle on the end table with a thud and rose to his feet.

Deacon walked to a side table and produced a pen and paper. "Just write it down," he said to Trevor.

Trevor scrutinized Callie as he passed, but thankfully he didn't say anything to her.

She was vaguely aware of Deacon seeing Trevor out, and then Deacon was back.

He dropped to one knee in front of her, concern in his expression. "What on earth?"

"They're *awful*." The words burst out of her, and she started to shake.

Deacon quickly took the mug from her hands and set it aside.

"All of them," she said. "They're mean and violent."

"Did he hurt you?"

"Not me. Not physically. Not much."

Deacon pulled her into his arms, holding her close.

She couldn't help herself. She tucked her head against his shoulder and closed her eyes, absorbing his strength as fear and dismay shuddered through her.

"I thought I was over it," she said.

"Tell me what happened."

Everything inside Deacon told him to go after Trevor. Whatever it was that Trevor had done to Callie in the past had hurt her badly. He should be held responsible. Deacon wanted justice for the way Callie was shaking in his arms.

But Callie needed him.

He eased her to one side of the big chair and sat down himself, drawing her into his lap, cradling her close and rubbing her arms.

"Tell me," he gently urged.

Whatever it was, he was going to make it better. Somehow, some way, he was going to make it better.

"How could they do that?" she asked, her voice a rasp. "How could they be so cruel? I was just a little girl."

He listened while she told him about the family's abject poverty. There was never enough money for food and clothes. She'd gone to school in castoffs from the church rummage sale. Their electricity was often turned off. They barely had heat, never mind air conditioning in the summer. And she'd slept for years on a damp mattress on the floor.

Meanwhile, she and her mother had waited on her father and brothers hand and foot, enduring shouts, curses and shoves. She told Deacon about the terror she felt when her parents fought, how her father slapped her mother, and how she'd been relieved when her father had died of a heart attack.

But her brothers hadn't let up. It wasn't until they finally left home, one by one, that she had any peace. Money was still tight, and then her mother got sick. At fourteen, she'd found a part-time job and tried desperately to hold it together financially. But then her mom died, and the hospital bills came due, and Callie had quit school.

While she spoke, her shaking slowly subsided. "Frederick was the first person to care for me. He was so kind. He was so gentle. I was never afraid of him."

She was a limp bundle of heat in Deacon's arms. Twin tear tracks glistened on her cheeks. Her hair was tousled, her legs were curled up.

"Have you ever told anyone about this?" he asked gently.

"There was no one to tell. Frederick had more problems than I could imagine."

"He had different problems."

"I couldn't tell him. I didn't want to tell him. It was in the past by then." She gave a shaky laugh. "I wanted to pretend it had happened to someone else. I wasn't her anymore, that defenseless little girl, exploited like a servant." She fell silent.

"I'm glad you told me." Deacon kissed her temple.

She sighed and rested her head against his shoulder.

He kissed away the tear track on her cheek. Her lips were dark and soft and sweet, and he gave in to temptation, kissing her tenderly, trying to will away her pain and heartache.

She kissed him back.

But then she gasped and turned her head away. "Deacon."

"I know," he said, wrapping his arms fully around her, holding her desperately close. "I won't let it get away from us. I promise."

"We can't."

"We won't." He rocked her. "Just let me hold you."

Minutes ticked past before he felt her relax.

He wanted to kiss her again, but he knew he'd be lost. And he couldn't let himself do that. She needed his comfort, not his lust.

He sat for an hour.

He didn't know exactly when she fell asleep, but she did.

He didn't want to put her down. He didn't want to let her go. But he had something to do, and he wasn't going to let it wait.

He carried her upstairs, laid her gently on her bed and pulled a comforter overtop of her.

Then he set his jaw, trotted down the stairs and took the paper with Trevor's phone number. He dialed as he walked to his car and opened the driver's door.

"Yo," Trevor answered, music twanging in the background.

"It's Deacon Holt." Deacon climbed in and shut the door, pressing the ignition button.

There was a brief pause on the line. "Well, Mr. Holt. That didn't take long."

"I want to meet," Deacon said, an adrenalin buzz energizing his system. He pictured Trevor in a seedy bar.

"Sure. Can do. When would you like this meeting?"

"Now. Where are you?"

There was another pause and a muttered voice. "It's called The Waterstreet Grill."

Deacon knew the place. It wasn't a dive. Too bad.

"I'll be there in ten minutes."

"You got it," Trevor said.

Deacon hung up the phone and pulled out of the driveway. It was after ten o'clock, so the roads were mostly clear. He lowered the windows and let the breeze flow in, trying to cool his temper. He kept picturing Trevor, who was six feet tall, shouting at a miniature Callie, her lugging cans of beer, and him chugging them down.

He smacked his hands on the steering wheel, swore out loud and pressed his foot on the accelerator. He made it to The Waterstreet Grill and swung into the curb out front. It was a no parking zone, but he really didn't care if they towed him.

He left the car, crossed the sidewalk and shoved open the heavy door.

It was dim inside the grill. The restaurant section was almost empty, but the bar was full. Country-pop came out of ceiling speakers, and cigarette smoke wafted in through an open door to the side alley.

He spotted Trevor talking with two other men at the bar. He made his way over.

"Yo, Deacon," Trevor said with a wide smile. He held up his hand to shake.

Deacon ignored it. He cocked his head toward the open door.

"You can talk in front of my friends," Trevor said. He clapped one of the men on the back. "This here's—"

"I don't want to talk in front of your friends," Deacon said.

Trevor's expression fell. "Chill, bro."

Deacon grimaced. "Shall we step outside?"

"Is this a fight?" Trevor asked with an uncomfortable laugh.

"No. But it can be." Deacon turned for the side door, confident that Trevor would follow.

Deacon passed two groups of smokers in the alley and went a few feet further.

"You're the one who called me," Trevor said as he caught up.

Deacon pivoted. "Callie is not your gravy train."

Trevor's eyes narrowed and crackled, his passive demeanor vanishing. "She's my sister. We're family."

"What you were to her isn't family."

"Got a birth certificate that says different."

"She owes you nothing."

"Let her tell me that."

Deacon stepped forward into Trevor's space. "You're never speaking to her again."

"Are you threatening me?"

Deacon reached into his jacket pocket and withdrew a check. He knew exactly why Trevor had come back into Callie's life, and he was taking the most direct route to sending him away.

"Consider this the carrot," he said, planting the check against Trevor's chest. "If it doesn't work, I've got a stick."

Trevor stepped back, grabbing at the check. He looked down, his widening eyes giving away his surprise at the amount.

"You're gone," Deacon said. "And you're never coming back."

"Is this good?" Trevor asked.

"Gone," Deacon repeated and turned to walk away.

He hoped he'd made his point.

Ten

James and Ethan looked adorable in their matching tuxes. James wore a red bowtie, while Ethan's was royal blue. Callie was a ridiculously proud mom.

Deacon looked magnificent, while Callie couldn't help but feel beautiful in her designer gown, with its glittering bodice, peekaboo back and flowing chiffon skirt. Deacon had insisted she buy it. And she'd been inclined to make him happy, since he'd been so supportive about Trevor.

Deacon said he had spoken to Trevor and promised her that her brother wouldn't be back. She hadn't asked Deacon what he'd said. She didn't care. It was enough that she didn't have the weight of her family hanging over her head.

"Mommy, Grandma gave us pudding," James said with excitement as he arrived holding Dee's hand.

"Mousse," Dee told Callie.

"Chocolate?" Callie asked.

"We were careful of their white shirts."

"It's nearly eight o'clock," Callie said. She didn't give the boys sugar, never mind chocolate, after five.

"Oh, don't worry so much," Margo said, arriving with a fluttery wave of her hand.

"We should probably take them home soon." Callie looked around for Deacon. She didn't mind driving the boys home on her own if he wanted to stay.

"What's the rush?" Margo asked.

"They'll be getting tired," Callie said.

"I'm not tired," James said.

"They're doing fine. Their grandpa and I still want to show them off."

Callie hesitated. The boys did seem to still have energy. It was probably the chocolate, but she understood Margo's perspective. She had gone to a lot of trouble for tonight.

"A little while," Callie agreed.

"I'll stay with them," Dee said.

"I can come along." Callie knew she should keep an eye on their moods.

"Don't be silly," Margo said. "Go find Deacon and have a dance."

In the face of the onslaught, Callie gave in. A selfish part of her did want to dance in her new gown. A foolish part of her wanted to dance with Deacon.

To do that, she'd have to throw caution to the wind.

She paused to give her saner side an opportunity to talk her out of it. Instead, she admitted this was a caution-to-the-wind kind of night. Her toddler had just eaten chocolate pudding at eight o'clock.

She caught sight of Deacon across the room.

He met her gaze and smiled.

She felt the attraction arc between them. She returned his smile and started toward him.

He must have seen something in her eyes, because he looked puzzled. Then he looked pleased, then he looked flat-out sexy.

"Dance?" she asked without giving herself a second to hesitate.

"Absolutely." He took her hand and led her toward the dance floor.

There was a small orchestra in the corner of the grand ballroom. The polished floor was smooth under her feet. Deacon's lead was sure, his steps perfect, his arm wonderful around her waist.

"This is some party," she said as they twirled across the floor.

"It's been a tradition for two hundred years."

She drew back. "Seriously?"

"The Clarksons are big on tradition. Take a look at the walls. Those are real swords and shields from the ancestors back home. The Clarksons came over on the Mayflower and fought in the civil war."

"Which side?"

"This is Virginia, ma'am. Both sides."

Callie grinned. "That's hedging your bets."

The music changed to a slower rhythm, and Deacon went quiet. His hand moved against the small of her back, gently stroking, his thumb touching the skin revealed by the open back of her dress.

She knew she shouldn't sink into the sensation, but she couldn't help herself. She shifted closer and closer, until she was flush against him. He put his cheek to her hair, and she burrowed into the crook of his neck.

Desire pulsed deep into her body. The music flowed

louder. Voices around them disappeared. The other dancers faded to a swirl of color.

Then she heard it, faint but unmistakable. It was Ethan's cry.

She jumped back from Deacon.

He seemed stunned. "What?"

"Ethan," she called. "Something's wrong." She rushed toward the sound.

"No," Ethan was shouting.

Callie rushed as fast as she could on her high heels.

She could see Margo talking to Ethan.

Ethan screwed up his face and shook his head.

Tyrell said something, and Ethan looked up. At first he looked scared, but then he dropped to the floor and squealed.

Tyrell reached down and pulled him back to his feet as Callie came within earshot.

"—and behave yourself!" Tyrell's tone was sharp.

Callie quickly crouched to put her arms around her son. "Sweetheart? What is it?"

Ethan started to cry.

She stood, wrapping him in her arms.

"I don't think coddling him will help," Tyrell said.

Callie glared at him. She didn't care that this was his house, and that he was the party's host. Ethan was her son, and her parenting choices were none of Tyrell's business.

This was all her fault, not Ethan's. It was nearly nine o'clock.

James was watching the whole thing with wide eyes.

She took his hand. "It's time for us to go home, honey."

"Oh, there's no need for that." Margo's tone was soothing.

Deacon arrived. "Is everything all right?"

Margo spoke directly to Deacon. It was the first time Callie had seen her do that.

"I was just telling Callie there's no need for her to leave early. We've set up the nursery for the boys."

Callie didn't want the nursery. She didn't want to stay here any longer. She wanted to take her boys home to their own beds.

"Ethan?" Dee came up close to him. "Would you like me to read you a story? You can have a bubble bath, too."

Callie didn't like the idea. "I think it's better if we—"

Ethan's voice was watery. "Which story?"

"The Pig and the Duck."

"The whole thing?" Ethan asked.

"I like *The Pig and the Duck*," James said. "And I like bubbles."

Ethan stopped crying and raised his head, looking at Callie.

"Do you want Dee to read you a story?" she asked.

Ethan nodded.

Deacon touched her shoulder and whispered in her ear. "It's completely up to you."

"There's a room made up for you, too," Margo said. "It's right across the hall from the nursery. You wouldn't have to disturb them at the end of the party."

Against her better judgement, Callie took the path of least resistance. They were only moments from the nursery. It would take at least half an hour to get the boys loaded into the car and back home. By the time they got there, Ethan would be truly miserable.

"Okay," she said. "Dee can put you to bed." She handed Ethan to Dee, who took James's hand to walk away.

"You shouldn't encourage that kind of behavior," Tyrell said to Callie.

"Don't," Deacon warned him. "Callie is a fantastic mother."

"It was the chocolate." Callie felt the need to defend Ethan. It might not have been his finest hour, but he wasn't the one to blame.

"Shall we dance again?" Deacon asked her.

She took him up on the offer. It might not be the smart thing, but she missed Deacon's arms, and she wanted to get away from Margo and Tyrell.

She knew Tyrell had a big personality, that he preferred things his own way, but this was the first time it had touched her personally. And on the heels of her brother's unsettling visit, it was more than she could take.

Deacon heard Callie open then close the bedroom door. She'd been across the hall, checking on James and Ethan, and now she set the baby monitor on a small table.

It was after midnight, and the party was quickly winding to a close. Although there were still dozens of guests, not to mention the staff, in the halls below, the castle walls were thick, and here on the second floor, it was completely quiet.

The room was large, with warm wooden walls, recessed windows showing the original stone structure, heavy ceiling beams and a thick woven carpet. There was a massive carved wood canopy bed in the center, flanked by two armchairs around a fireplace and a small table and chair set. The walk-in closet and the connected bathroom were at opposite ends of the room.

Callie looked tired but beautiful in her flowing gown. Her upswept hair was wispy around her face, and when she reached down to strip off her high heels, Deacon felt a surge of desire. It was pathetic, really, finding her bare feet that sexy.

"Are the boys okay?" he asked as a conversation opener. He didn't want to address the sleeping arrangements head on.

"Did it seem weird to you?" she asked. "Earlier, I mean." She looked around the floor, settling on putting her shoes beneath the upholstered bench positioned at the foot of the bed.

"Did what seem weird?" All Deacon remembered was holding her in his arms on the dance floor, watching her talk and smile with the other guests, not being able to take his gaze off her all night long.

"Margo with the boys. I mean, Tyrell was a jerk. I don't want him alone with the boys, especially Ethan."

"I understand." Deacon had no intention of letting Tyrell babysit.

"But Margo." Callie perched on the bench. "Does she seem a bit possessive to you?"

"She adores her grandsons." That had been obvious to Deacon from minute one.

"That nursery." Callie pointed across the hall. "It's full of toys and clothes. They could live there forever if they wanted."

Deacon moved closer to Callie. "The Clarksons do have a lot of money."

She tipped her chin to look up. "I know. It's just a funny feeling I get around her lately. She called Ethan *Beau*. James told me that."

"They do look alike."

"Yeah. You're right. I guess it's not that strange."

"Are you okay staying here?" he asked.

"It doesn't make any sense to wake the boys up."

Deacon looked meaningfully to the big bed, the only place in the room for either of them to sleep. "I mean…"

It seemed to occur to her for the first time. "Oh." She

drew a sigh. "I'm so exhausted, I don't even care. Will it bother you?"

"Not in the least." He was surprised by her pragmatic acceptance.

She sized up the bed again. "I doubt we could find each other if we tried."

He'd find her in about half a second. But he wouldn't.

He'd already hung up his jacket, and now he stripped off his tie. As he removed his white shirt, her gaze seemed to stall on his chest. He wanted it to mean something, but he doubted it did.

He held out the shirt. "Here."

"What?"

"You can sleep in this."

She blinked. She paused. "Oh. Okay. Thanks."

He gestured to the bathroom. "Go ahead."

She rose and took the shirt.

She shut the door behind her, and a vision of her changing bloomed in his mind. To distract himself, he removed his shoes and set them next to hers. Then he pulled the curtains on four separate windows. He flicked on a bedside lamp and turned off the overhead lights.

He turned down the bed and fluffed the pillows, folding the heavy spread and laying it across the bench at the foot of the bed.

The bathroom door opened, and Callie emerged. He told himself not to look. It was going to kill him. But he couldn't help himself.

She was backlit, his white shirt slightly translucent, falling to her mid-thigh, the sleeves rolled up along her slender arms, the top button open to make a V-neck.

The world seemed to stop.

"Is there a hanger…?" She removed the gown from

a hook inside the door, the motion bringing his shirt against her breasts.

He nearly groaned out loud.

"The closet's over here," he managed.

She draped the gown over her arms.

"I can get that." He quickly took the gown from her arms.

"Thank you."

It took all his strength not to touch her, not to hold her like he had on the dance floor. Her green eyes met his in the shadowy light. She'd scrubbed off her makeup, and there was a fresh glow to her skin.

She was so incredibly, naturally beautiful. And she'd once told him she loved him.

But he'd ruined all that. Right now, he'd have done anything to rewind time, to fix his mistakes, to find a way back to where they'd been in Charleston.

Instead, he had to find a way to keeps his hands off her.

"Deacon," she said in a tentative voice.

"I can do this," he vowed on a whisper.

She looked at the dress, obviously misunderstanding his words.

He gave himself a mental shake. "Go to bed," he told her softly. "You should sleep."

She nodded.

While he hung the gown, she climbed under the covers.

Deacon shut off the bathroom light, stripped to his boxers and joined her, lastly turning the switch on the bedside lamp and plunging the room into darkness.

The blankets rustled, and he felt her move.

"I don't like it here," she said.

"Do you want me to leave?"

There was a short silence. “No. I mean I don’t like this place, the castle. It feels, I don’t know, dark.”

“It is dark.” He couldn’t see his hand in front of his face.

He wondered if he’d made a mistake in drawing all the curtains. If the boys woke up, he and Callie would probably trip on the furniture getting to them.

“I mean somber. It feels like the walls want to suck the very joy out of life.”

“It is cold and hard. Funny, from the outside it always looked grand.”

“It’s grand on the inside, too.”

“It has no soul.”

“That’s it,” she said.

He couldn’t see her, but he heard her come up on her elbow. He did the same, facing her in the dark, barely able to discern her outline as his eyes adjusted.

“Do you think it could be haunted?” There was a joking note to her voice.

“By eight generations of Clarksons?” He gave a chuckle. “Now there’s a daunting thought.”

“Would you protect me?”

“From the ghost of Admiral Frederick Baines Clarkson?” Deacon deepened his voice, speaking with exaggerated drama. “Legend has it that Admiral Clarkson was murdered.”

She matched his tone. “Here in the walls of Clarkson Castle?”

“I believe we may be in mortal danger.” He gave a pause, glancing around at the tiny rays of light below the curtains. “Shh. Do you hear that?”

The wind was blowing through the battlements.

“Are you trying to scare me?”

"It's his ship's whistle. He's calling his men, still angry they didn't save him."

"You have a vivid imagination." She batted her hand against his shoulder.

The second she touched him, his world stopped.

She stopped.

Then she moved.

Her hand smoothed over his skin, to his neck, to his cheek.

"Callie," he breathed in desperation. "I can't… I won't…"

"I know," she said. "It's…" She shifted closer. Her breath brushed his face. Her lips touched his.

His reaction was immediate. His arm went around her waist, he pressed her into the soft mattress, his mouth opened wide, his kiss went deep. Every sense he had zeroed in on Callie.

Her hand burrowed into his hair, anchoring. Her arm wound around his neck. Their bodies came tight together, and he absorbed her heat, her softness, her essence.

He kissed her mouth over and over again.

Then he moved to her neck, her shoulders, her breasts.

She gasped his name.

He stripped off her shirt, kicked off his boxers, and they clung naked to each other, limbs entwined. He breathed in her essence, tasted her skin, felt the softness of her lavender-scented hair between his fingertips.

"I've missed you so much," he rasped.

"Oh, Deacon." There was a catch in her voice.

He reached beneath her, tilting her body toward him. Her thighs softly parted. Her legs went around him.

He stopped, poised, holding himself back, wanting the magic to go on forever.

"Deacon, please," she moaned, and he plunged them together.

Her breaths pulsed against him. He kissed her deeply. He cradled her breasts, smoothed the backs of her thighs, captured her body, her core, over and over again.

Her arms convulsed around him, and her hips surged to meet him. Their passion heated the air of the cold castle. The thick walls absorbed their cries. The darkness cocooned them, and every shadow of his heritage disappeared.

The past didn't matter, only the future. And the future was Callie. It had to be Callie.

Her body contracted, pulling him over the edge, and he spiraled irrevocably into paradise.

Coming back home the next day, Callie realized how much she loved Deacon's house. It was welcoming, comfortable and functional. It was roomy, but really just the right size. The kitchen was brilliantly laid out, with every convenience. She could clean up from lunch while watching the boys play with building bricks in the family room.

It had been Deacon's idea to add a toy box to the family room décor. So the boys could play and easily help clean up afterward. She was even getting used to a housekeeper twice a week. She was over the guilt of having someone else dust, vacuum and scrub her shower.

Now Deacon appeared by her side. She knew he'd been in his study making calls. He'd mentioned he was at odds with Beau over something, and he was trying to put together his own side of the argument. She'd learned he worked seven days a week. He might dial it back a bit on the weekends, but the port never closed, so there was always some problem to be solved.

He gave her a gentle touch on the shoulder. Still on a

high from last night, she simply enjoyed the feeling. She'd have to come back down to earth soon. She couldn't simply pretend their marriage had turned normal. But not today—she wasn't going to let reality intrude just yet.

"I thought I'd take them outside for a while," Deacon said. "Maybe run around with the soccer ball and burn off some energy."

"I'm all for that," she said.

"Do you want to take a nap?"

She couldn't help but think the offer was a veiled reference to how little sleep she'd had last night. She'd slept in Deacon's arms, but mostly they'd made love and talked and made love some more. He'd said he missed her. She missed him more than she could have imagined.

"I'm fine," she said now. She really was. There was a spring in her step and energy in her veins.

"I think I'll call Hannah."

"Whatever you want." Deacon gave her a quick kiss on the temple and helped himself to the leftover cheese. "Who wants to play soccer?" he called to the boys.

Ethan jumped to his feet. "Soccer, soccer!"

"I need my red runners," James said.

"Let's gear up." Deacon swung Ethan up on his shoulders, giving Callie a parting wink as they headed for the foyer.

She returned the cold cuts to the refrigerator and wiped down the counter.

After stacking the dishes in the dishwasher, she took the kitchen phone and wandered onto the sundeck, where she could see Deacon and the boys playing on the far side of the yard. The sunshine was warm, and she stretched out on a padded lounger in her shorts and T-shirt. She put on a pair of sunglasses against the glare and dialed the bakery.

"Good afternoon, Downright Sweet Bakery." It was Hannah's voice.

"Are you busy?" Callie asked.

"Callie! Hi! How are you?"

Callie could hear the familiar sounds of the lunch crowd in the background. "I don't want to interrupt."

"It's steady but not bad."

The sounds faded as Hannah obviously moved into the back, probably into the office.

"I just wanted to check in," Callie said.

"It's turning into a good summer. Tourist business has been steady. The city rose garden is under construction. There wasn't another word about putting it at Fifth and Bay Street. I don't know what you said to the Mayor."

"It was Deacon."

"Well, he's magic."

Callie knew the magic was really Deacon's check book. She didn't like it, but she'd gotten over it. The important thing was that business was going well for Hannah.

"Speaking of the Mayor," Hannah said. "He has a serious challenger for re-election."

"I thought he was going for governor."

"Ha! That didn't pan out. Rumor has it his opponent has the support of two Congress Members and some financial backers."

Callie was afraid to hear the details. One thing she'd learned was that she wanted no part of the backroom power and deception, or the deals and betrayals, which often came along with politics.

"So long as he's staying away from you," she said to Hannah.

"Far away. We started a new product line this week."

"Do tell."

"I found a steady source of haskap berries in Colorado. They're supposed to be a superfood, all the rage and a wonderful color and flavor. We've done a muffin, a rainbow lemon loaf and syrup for the vanilla cheesecake."

"I can't wait to try them."

"How are the boys?"

"They're good." Callie focused on the soccer game. "They're kicking a ball around in the backyard with Deacon."

"He's super. You got yourself a great guy there, Callie."

"Yes," she managed. There were so many things about Deacon that were great.

If he hadn't lied about who he was, what he wanted, and his feelings for her, things would be downright perfect. Her heart hollowed out as she watched him laughing with James, passing the ball to Ethan. It was heartbreaking that it all had to end.

"Not yet," she whispered.

"What was that?" Hannah asked.

"Nothing. He's great." Callie could ignore his flaws, at least for a little while.

In the early morning, before Tyrell and Beau arrived in the business wing of the castle, Deacon sought Aaron out in his office. Tyrell occupied the large CEO's office in the corner, beside the boardroom. Tyrell's assistant and three other staff members worked in a common area outside. Aaron, Beau and now Deacon had offices along the north wall, overlooking the harbor and the port in the distance.

"I've fleshed out some more details," Deacon told Aaron, setting a file folder on his deck.

"The vertical integration?" Aaron asked.

"Yes."

"I thought you gave up on that."

"Why would I give up on it? It's a solid solution."

"Because without either Beau or my father's support, it's a nonstarter." But Aaron did open the folder.

"Tyrell might come around," Deacon said.

"You don't know him very well."

Deacon couldn't argue with that. Aaron knew both Beau and Tyrell far better than Deacon did. Aaron was probably right. But Deacon had to try.

Things were going so much better with Callie, that Deacon was beginning to see a future with her: a future with her, a future with the Clarksons and a future managing Hale Harbor Port—both for him and for James and Ethan.

That meant he had to take a long view, to push for what was best. Even if the odds were stacked against him, he had to try.

Aaron was his best bet. Aaron was smart. He was methodical. He wasn't anything like his hotheaded brother, Beau.

Aaron thumbed through the top sheets. "How optimistic are these numbers?"

"They're realistic. We've done a low, medium and high case scenario."

"It might be a range, but it's still only speculative."

Deacon was prepared for the question. "The base data was derived from—"

"Is this a private meeting?" Tyrell's tone from the open doorway was clearly a rebuke.

Deacon had learned Tyrell was an exacting man, a cantankerous man and also a paranoid man.

Aaron closed the file. "Volumetric data and route statistics."

It wasn't a lie, but it wasn't the full truth either. Deacon appreciated Aaron's discretion. It also told him Aaron wasn't completely opposed to pursing the idea of vertical integration. That was encouraging.

"I need to talk to you," Tyrell said to Deacon.

"Sure." Deacon left the file with Aaron in the hopes that he'd read further.

He followed Tyrell to his office, where Tyrell shut the door after them. Tyrell took his position behind the massive dark walnut desk. Beyond him were big recessed windows, the glass so old, it warped the city and mountains behind.

Sounds echoed in the big room, because unlike most of the rest of the castle, Tyrell had not covered the stone walls with paneling. Instead, he'd covered them with vintage oil paintings and coats of arms. The stone floor was worn, and the guest chairs were red velvet and ornate wood, anything but comfortable.

Tyrell sat down, and so did Deacon.

"You've had time to settle in," Tyrell said.

"I have."

"And Callie? And the boys?"

"Them, too." Deacon couldn't help but be curious about where this was going.

It wasn't like Tyrell to ask after anyone's welfare.

"It's been nearly a month," he said.

"Not quite," Deacon said. He was acutely aware of time passing, as he worried about Callie's ultimate decision to stay or go.

"Nevertheless," Tyrell said.

Deacon waited.

"It's time to make some changes."

Deacon's senses went on alert. "Changes to what?"

"To your circumstance. Margo and I have discussed it, and we want you to move into the castle."

The request gave Deacon a jolt. "That was never part of the deal."

And it wasn't something Deacon would ever consider. For one thing, Callie would hate it. For another, Deacon valued his independence far too much. And most importantly, it wouldn't be good for James and Ethan. Deacon planned to keep their exposure to Tyrell at an absolute minimum.

"It's not negotiable," Tyrell said.

"I wasn't planning to negotiate with you. The answer is no. We're not moving into the castle. I don't even know why you'd want us here. Margo can barely stand to look at me."

"That's not her fault."

"No, it's your fault."

"Nevertheless," Tyrell said.

"*Nevertheless* is not a rational argument for anything."

"You *will* move in."

"What part of *no* is getting past you?"

"What part of *will* is getting past *you*?"

"You can't force the issue," Deacon said. "You can't undo the contract. The shares are mine."

Deacon's lawyer had assured him that Tyrell could not renege on the contract.

"That may be true." Tyrell sat forward, bracing his hands on the desk. "But I have the power to change the class of your shares."

Deacon narrowed his eyes, focusing on Tyrell's unyielding expression, trying to imagine where this threat was going.

"With a two-thirds majority vote, I can change your shares from Class A to Class D. That means no voting rights, no position in the company, no dividends. Your interest in the company would be effectively worthless."

Deacon held his composure, refusing to let Tyrell see the news rattled him. Tyrell wouldn't be bluffing. Somehow, in the hundreds of pages of the contract agreement, Tyrell's lawyers had planted a loophole.

"I could sell," Deacon said.

There was nothing Tyrell could do to make the shares completely worthless. And Deacon could throw a wrench in the works by threatening to sell to someone hostile.

"You're forgetting the buyback clause. Hale Harbor Port would be happy to reacquire the shares at the price you paid for them."

"I would sue."

Tyrell laughed at that. "My dear boy, you can try. But you will lose. It will take years and the legal fees would break you."

Deacon clenched his jaw. He racked his brain, but he didn't immediately see another option. And deep down, he knew Tyrell's army of lawyers would have thought through every strategy.

Tyrell truly had no soul.

"I gave you everything you wanted," Deacon said. Though his effort was most certainly doomed, he had to try to reason with Tyrell.

"I wanted my grandsons."

"And they're here."

"No. They're not *here*. They're with you."

"They're with their mother."

"And she can live here."

"She won't agree to it." Deacon was completely sure of that. She'd probably walk out the minute he asked her.

"That's *your* problem," Tyrell said.

He took a pen from the ornate holder in front of him,

slipped on his reading glasses and pointedly picked up a report.

"And if I can't convince her to do it?" Deacon asked.

Tyrell peered over the top of his glasses. "Then I convert your shares."

Deacon came to his feet. "You're the real bastard in this family."

"Is that a yes?"

"It looks as though I have no choice."

A smirk twitched Tyrell's mouth. "I'm glad you see things my way."

Eleven

Callie's heart sank as she stared at her brother Trevor in the doorway. Deacon had promised her Trevor wouldn't be back. And she'd believed him.

The boys were playing on the staircase behind her, building jumps for their little race cars.

"You shouldn't be here," Callie said to Trevor.

She felt instantly alone and vulnerable. Deacon wouldn't be home for hours.

"You're gonna want to hear what I have to say," Trevor drawled.

"No, I don't." She started to close the door.

He blocked it with a stiff arm, and her heart thudded hard against her chest.

"What do you want?" she asked, hating the fear in her voice.

"I want to know your game."

"What game? There is no game. Just go, Trevor."

"He paid me off. He paid me good."

Callie hadn't known Deacon had bribed Trevor. But it shouldn't have surprised her. At the moment, she was even grateful.

"So go away. You got what you came for."

Trevor gave a cold laugh. He unexpectedly shoved the door open and walked inside.

James and Ethan both looked up.

"Are these the little tykes?"

"James, take Ethan to the family room. You can watch cartoons."

Trevor moved toward them. "No need for them to skedaddle."

Callie's fear for her own safety evaporated, and she bolted between her brother and her sons. "James, honey, take Ethan. You can each have a cookie while you watch."

"Candy cookies," Ethan sang.

"Okay, Mommy."

"Thank you, sweetheart." She glared at Trevor and listened as the boys left the foyer behind her. "What do you want?" she demanded.

"More of the same."

"Deacon's not going to give you more money."

Trevor took a few steps across the foyer, his black boots glaring against the polished white tile. "I met a guy at the bar, a new drinking buddy of mine."

Callie kept herself between Trevor and the hallway that led to the family room.

"He's a gardener down there at that castle. Word is out on your scam, baby sister."

"I don't know what you're talking about." She wanted him out. She wasn't exactly afraid anymore, but she wanted Trevor out of the house.

"Oh, you know exactly what I'm talkin' about. The two of you are taking that family for millions."

She'd had enough. She marched back to the door and pulled it wide. "Get out."

"Not a chance."

"There is no scam," she said.

Trevor moved closer. "Then why's Deacon never been to the castle before? Why'd nobody even speak his name until he showed up with you? Now he's got the run of the place. Because of your kids." Trevor cast his gaze toward the family room.

"They're Tyrell's grandchildren," she said. "It's not a scam."

"Then it's a bribe," Trevor said with conviction. "And I want in on the action."

"It's not a—"

The word *bribe* echoed ominously inside Callie's head.

Bribes were Deacon's go-to tool. He did it all the time.

"You bribed the old man," Trevor said.

Callie hadn't bribed anyone. But had Deacon? Could Deacon have used the boys to worm his way into the Clarkson family?

If he had, everything suddenly made sense.

Deacon's voice boomed through the room. "What are you doing here?" He grasped Trevor by the collar and hustled him onto the porch.

Trevor only barely kept his footing. "Hey, man, I'm—"

"You're trespassing on private property." Deacon slammed the door in Trevor's face. He whirled to Callie. "Are you all right? Where are the kids?"

"Am I a bribe?" she asked, her voice quavering.

The enormity of what Trevor had just accused Deacon of, and the reality that he could be right, had shaken her to the core.

"What?" Deacon looked dumfounded.

"Trevor said—"

"You're listening to *Trevor*?"

"He said you bribed your way into the Clarkson family, using me and the boys."

The expression on Deacon's face told her it was true.

She gasped and took two steps backward.

He reached for her.

"No! That explains it all. It explains everything. You finding me, pretending to like me, lying to me, manipulating me."

"You have to listen, Callie."

"I don't. I really don't."

James came running through the foyer with his arms outstretched, as he made airplane noises.

Ethan followed in the same posture. "Hi, Daddy."

The two of them did a loop and left again.

"What have you done?" Callie whispered through a throat closing with emotion.

"Tyrell came to me with the offer. He promised me my birthright, and I was tempted. I admit, I was tempted. It was everything I ever wanted in my life. Everything."

"You took it," she said. "You *took* it."

"No. I didn't. I only agreed to meet you."

"You lied to me and married me, and brought us home like some prize."

"By then I thought you wanted to marry me. I thought you had your own agenda."

"Your money," she said woodenly. "Yeah, I remember that lie, too."

"It all went horribly wrong," he said.

"Not for you. For you, it all went horribly right."

He turned from her and raked a hand through his hair. "Not anymore."

She didn't need to listen to this. She needed to get her boys, pack her things, get out of Hale Harbor and never come back.

Deacon was a liar, and she was never going to see him again. Ever.

Her heart shouldn't hurt this much.

"He wants us to live at the castle," Deacon said.

Callie mutely shook her head. No way, no how. That was *not* going to happen.

"He gave me an ultimatum today. I move you to the castle, or I lose it all."

"They want the boys," she found herself whispering. "They're trying to steal my sons."

"I told him yes."

"What?"

"Only to buy us some time. I came home to tell you everything. And to tell you, you need to leave."

James and Ethan buzzed through, playing airplane again.

"I *am* leaving," she said as her sons trotted out of earshot.

"Today. Right now," Deacon said. "I was going to tell you everything that happened, and then tell you to take the boys, take them to Charleston and never come back. I made a deal with the devil, and I was wrong."

"*Yes*, you were wrong!"

"Thing is…" he said, his tone turning reflective.

She refused to listen. "There's no *thing*. There is nothing."

"I kept trying to stay logical, to stay detached."

"Bully for you." She hadn't had the opportunity to stay logical and detached, because she'd been conned from minute one.

"But I couldn't."

"Stop talking."

"It took me way too long to recognize it, but I fell in love with you."

What was left of her heart shattered into pieces.

"You can't do that," she cried. "You can't say that. You can't wait until after everything else has failed and then throw that out on the table."

"I know."

"You can't."

"I can't. And I won't. Callie, I'm so sorry I let you down."

If the banging on the front door hadn't been so insistent, Deacon wouldn't have bothered answering. The house was eerily quiet with Callie and the boys gone. It had been less than twenty-four hours, and Deacon hadn't yet decided how to move forward.

This morning, he'd found one of Ethan's socks under a sofa cushion. He'd stared at it for a long time, trying to decide whether to wash it and mail it to Charleston or toss it out. Right now, it was sitting on a table in the family room, while he made up his mind.

Through the prismed window of his front door, he recognized Aaron. Deacon didn't particularly want to talk to him, but he didn't care enough to make an issue of it either. He'd rather face Aaron now and send him away than risk him coming back later and disturbing Deacon all over again.

Deacon opened the door.

He was shocked to see Beau standing next to his brother.

"What are you doing here?" he asked them bluntly.

"We want to talk," Aaron said.

Deacon coughed out a laugh of disbelief. “We’ve got nothing to talk about.”

“I think we do,” Beau said.

Deacon took in their determined stares. He didn’t care enough to fight this either. He stepped back. “Come on in.”

They glanced at each other, then stepped into the foyer.

The library was closest, but it was a small room, too intimate for Deacon’s liking. He led them back to the living room, with its generous size, cavernous ceilings and huge bank of windows. Whatever they had to say could get lost in the space.

He gestured to a burgundy leather sofa and took the armchair across from it, putting a wide glass-topped table between them.

“We brought you something,” Aaron said, placing a document on the table.

“You don’t expect me to sign off on converting the shares.” Deacon couldn’t believe they had the nerve to show up and ask that. He was beginning to work up the energy to fight.

“It’s not the shares,” Aaron said. “After the last time you and I discussed vertical integration, I did some research.”

“Why are you telling me this? I’m out. You both know I’m out.”

“Will you listen?” Beau barked.

“Shut up,” Aaron told his brother.

“He makes everything difficult,” Beau said.

“You can leave anytime,” Deacon told Beau.

“I remembered something Frederick worked on six years ago.” Aaron pointed to the document. “It’s dated, but it has a lot of the same ideas you had. It even mentions Mobi Transportation. Back then, Frederick suggested bringing you into the family fold."

Deacon tried to make sense of that statement.

"Now he's listening," Beau said.

"Frederick didn't even know me," Deacon said.

"He knew of you. He went off to college and came back with a sense of social justice and some big ideas for the port. He shared them with Father, who crushed him like a bug. Father called Frederick *pathetic*."

Beau sat forward. "But Frederick stood up to him. He said we had to modernize, and he said it was the family's responsibility to include you, because you were Father's son. Father went ballistic."

Deacon was speechless.

"I should have stood up for him back then," Aaron said.

"*We* should have stood up for him back then," Beau said.

"He was right about modernizing," Aaron said. "And he was right about you."

"That's why he walked out?" Deacon asked, trying to wrap his mind around it.

"He had more guts than either of us," Beau said.

"We didn't stand up for Frederick," Aaron said. "We're not going to make the same mistake again. Not with our long-lost brother."

Deacon couldn't believe he'd heard right.

But Beau came to his feet and stuck his hand out to shake. "We're with you in this, brother. We want to stand together."

Deacon rose, and so did Aaron.

"I'm out," Deacon said. "Didn't Tyrell tell you? I won't move to the castle, so he's converting my shares."

"Callie can't move to the castle," Aaron said.

"No kidding," Deacon said.

"Miranda's wanted to leave for a while now," Aaron said. "She's tired of dealing with Mother and Father all the time. I didn't have it in me before, but I do now. We're moving out."

"Well, I'm not staying there by myself," Beau said.

"What will the old man do?" Deacon asked Aaron.

"He can't do anything if we stick together."

"Are we going to shake on this?" Beau asked, sticking his hand out more firmly.

Deacon shook. "I'm flattered. I'm really overwhelmed." His emotions couldn't seem to sort themselves out. "But, like I said, it's too late."

Aaron smiled. He shook Deacon's hand then added his other hand overtop. "You haven't been paying attention." Aaron paused for what looked like effect. "Tyrell needs a two-thirds majority to convert your shares. We won't give it to him."

Beau pointed around the circle at the three of them. "And between us, we've got more than two-thirds."

Deacon could not believe what he was hearing.

"We're in favor of vertical integration," Aaron said. "Want to come with us and tell Dad?"

"We?" Deacon started speaking slowly. "The three of us? We're going up against Tyrell?"

"He's traveling, but will be back in two days," Aaron said. "I think we should do this in person. You in?"

"He's going to flip." Beau grinned as he said it.

"Where's Callie?" Aaron asked, glancing around.

"She moved back to Charleston."

Beau frowned. "Why?"

"She left." Deacon saw no point in hiding the truth. "She didn't like being used as a pawn. She particularly didn't like me exploiting her children for personal gain."

Aaron looked confused. "But I thought the two of you were..."

"Not so much," Deacon said, fighting to hide his despair.

"Man, I'm going to miss those little guys," Beau said.

Deacon missed them so much, he could barely breathe.

And Callie, Callie...

He might have his birthright and two new brothers, and he was grateful for both of those things. But none of it made up for losing Callie.

He'd made mistake after mistake. He'd hurt her badly, and he deserved his misery.

Being back at the bakery was surreal for Callie. In some ways, the past two months seemed like a dream—a breathtaking, bewildering, heartbreaking dream.

Her chest was hollow where her heart used to be, but everything else was normal. She looked the same. She talked the same. She acted the same. And the world around her hadn't changed at all.

Hannah nudged her elbow, and Callie realized she was standing at the counter, staring off into space, while a customer waited for service.

"Nancy?" Hannah prompted, gesturing to the customer.

Nancy stepped up to help.

In the meantime, Hannah reached into the display case and extracted two oversize vanilla cupcakes with mountains of buttercream and caramel sprinkles.

"We need to talk," she said to Callie.

"About what?" Callie asked.

"This way." Cupcakes on plates, Hannah headed around the end of the counter, into the dining area.

When Callie joined her at a corner table, Hannah

handed her a fork and pushed one of the cupcakes in front of her.

"If ever there was a woman in need of buttercream..." Hannah said.

Callie had to admit, the cupcake looked unusually appealing. "I haven't had one of these in a very long time." She took a forkful of the rich, fluffy frosting and lifted it to her mouth.

"You haven't been this despondent in a very long time," Hannah said, digging into her own cupcake.

"I'm not despondent." Callie thought she was putting on a very brave front, especially considering how she felt inside.

Deacon was out of her life. It had only been three days, but it felt like a year. She'd lost count of the times James and Ethan had asked about Deacon.

Hannah's expression was full of sympathy. "What really happened?"

"It didn't work out." Callie had decided to keep her explanation simple.

"You were head over heels for that guy."

Callie felt her eyes mist up, and she covered her emotions with a bite of cupcake.

Hannah waited.

"It was a mistake," Callie said.

"It's never a mistake to fall in love."

"It is with the wrong guy."

Hannah tilted her head, her puzzlement clear. "Deacon was the right guy. He wasn't Hank, he wasn't—"

"He was worse than Hank." The words were out before Callie could think better of them.

"You're going to have to explain that." Hannah's tone was gentle but implacable.

Callie stopped eating. Her stomach couldn't take it.

"It was a con, Hannah. It was all a ruse." Once she started, she couldn't seem to stop herself. "Deacon's biological father, the rich and infamous Tyrell Clarkson—Frederick's father, too, by the way."

Hannah slowly set down her fork.

"Frederick was legitimate, but Deacon wasn't. Frederick hated his father, so he never told me anything about his family. I'm glad he didn't. It was the right decision to keep us apart. It would have been better if I'd never met any of them. But then Tyrell promised Deacon a share of the family fortune if he brought me back to Hale Harbor."

"How big of a share?"

"*That's* your question?"

Hannah gave a shrug. "Don't you wonder how much it took?"

"It was a lot."

"Millions?"

"Hundreds of millions."

Hannah's brow shot up.

"I suppose it's good to know I'm worth that much." Callie gave a slightly hysterical laugh, quickly covering her mouth. "It wasn't so much me. It was the boys. Tyrell's grandsons. His only grandchildren."

Hannah's palm went to her chest. "Oh, Callie. Deacon only pretended to love you?"

Callie gave a miserable nod.

"I'm so sorry."

"He told me he didn't love me."

"That's brutal."

"It was…" Callie's brain flashed a kaleidoscope of Deacon. "And then…in the end…when it was all falling apart, he even used that as a tactic."

"I don't understand."

Callie felt her misery turn to bitterness. "When Deacon couldn't deliver, when he couldn't get me to move the boys to the castle, Tyrell pulled out the rug. He took back Deacon's share of the company. And at that point, Deacon said he loved me." She snapped her fingers in the air. "Suddenly, he'd fallen in love with me."

"The castle?"

Callie gave a small shudder at the memory. "The Clarksons have an actual castle. You should have seen it. It's positively medieval. I could never in a thousand years live there."

As she spoke, her mind was drawn back to the night she'd spent in Deacon's arms, making such sweet sexy love with him in that castle. Their whispered conversations, the laughter, his warmth, his scent, his taste—for those few short hours, she thought it was going to work out. She thought they could make a life together.

"Callie?" Hannah interrupted Callie's memories. "You zoned out on me there."

Callie dragged herself back to reality. "It was nothing but a ruse."

"He admitted he didn't love you."

"Yes." Callie picked up her fork and determinedly dug into the cupcake again. She wasn't going to let Deacon, or anyone else, ruin buttercream.

"But then he said he did," Hannah confirmed.

"Only to get me to the castle."

"Walk me through it."

"What do you mean?" Callie asked.

"I'm trying to figure out why he'd change his story."

"It's simple. When Tyrell said 'move her to the castle or lose all the money,' Deacon suddenly decided he'd loved me all along."

"So he tried to convince you to move to the castle?"

"No." Callie cast her mind back to the conversation.

"He told me to take the boys to Charleston and never come back."

She went over it a second time in case her memory was flawed. But that was how it had happened.

"Before or after he told you he loved you?" Hannah asked.

"Before. It was before."

"So, he'd already given up the money." Sounding like she'd made an important point, Hannah scooped a bite of her cupcake.

"No. He still had the option of getting me to change my mind."

"Which he didn't do. You said he didn't even try."

In the strictest sense, Callie knew that was true. But it was more complicated than that. "He didn't bother, because he knew it was hopeless."

"That's not what I'm hearing."

"What are you hearing?"

"I'm hearing he gave up hundreds of millions. He told you to go back to Charleston. *Then* he told you he loved you."

"Which, *believe me*, if I'd let it, would have led to a pitch to move me to the castle."

"Maybe," Hannah said, sounding unconvinced.

"I was there."

"You were upset."

That was true enough. Callie didn't think she'd ever felt more upset in her life. Trevor's revelation had rocked her to her core. She hadn't told Hannah about Trevor. She tried to calculate how that would change the situation.

"You don't know what might have happened," Hannah said, polishing off her cupcake. "Eat."

"I know what *did* happen."

"Eat," Hannah said.

Callie took a bite.

"When you finish that cupcake," Hannah said. "I want you to consider that a man who gives up hundreds of millions of dollars for your well-being, then tells you he loves you, might…in fact…"

Callie couldn't let her mind go there. She couldn't survive another fantasy, another disappointment, another heartbreak.

"Love you," Hannah finished.

Callie took another bite of the cupcake, and another, and another, until it was gone.

"Well?" Hannah said.

"I can't go back. I can't let myself hope…" Callie wanted so desperately to hope, but she knew the stakes were far too high. She'd never survive another heartbreak.

"Then don't go back," Hannah said.

Callie was surprised. She was also a little disappointed. She realized she wanted Hannah to talk her into going to Deacon. That was beyond frightening.

"Call him. Text him."

"And say what?" It was the most preposterous idea Callie had ever heard.

"Anything. Text: *What's up? Where are you? What are you doing?* All you need is an icebreaker."

"I'm not doing that."

"Then text: *Can we talk?* If I'm right, he'll be on the next plane. If I'm wrong, he'll send some lame brush off answer, and you'll know for sure."

"He wouldn't have to wait for the next plane." Callie couldn't believe she was considering it. "He'd charter his own."

* * *

Tyrell swaggered into the boardroom, his expression dark. "What's this?" he demanded of Deacon, Aaron and Beau.

Deacon's phone pinged.

"We have some information to share with you," Aaron said.

Deacon watched Tyrell's suspicions rise. Deacon didn't feel the slightest sense of satisfaction or vindication. But he did feel a sense of justice.

His phone pinged again, and he glanced down.

His heart stopped when he saw Callie's name. Everything in the room disappeared.

He focused on her message.

Can we talk? her text said.

Yes, they could talk. Of course they could talk. They absolutely could talk. He came to his feet, pushing the chair out behind him.

"Deacon?" Aaron's voice penetrated.

Deacon looked up to three expressions of astonishment.

"I have to go," he said.

"What?" Beau demanded.

"I'm..." Deacon started for the door. "I'll...talk later. I have to go."

He all but sprinted down the hall. He didn't know what would happen in the boardroom behind him, but he didn't particularly care.

He texted while he walked: I'm on my way. Where are you?

He hopped into his car, tossing his phone on the passenger seat, watching it to see her answer. It was taking too long. It was taking way too long for her to respond.

He stopped at a light and picked up the phone, thinking something had gone wrong. He'd have to resend.

But then it pinged: At the bakery. But on my way home.

He glanced at the red light and typed in a message: *Be there in an hour.*

A horn honked behind him. He hit send and switched to hands free, contacting an air charter company.

They had a jet with immediate availability. He didn't ask the price, all but threw them his credit card in the boarding lounge and leapt on board.

He barely noticed the opulent white leather surroundings. He did say yes to a single malt, hoping it would calm his nerves. The pilot was able to radio ahead for a car, and Deacon came close to his time estimate.

One hour and twenty minutes later, he was at Callie's front door.

She opened it, and he had to fight an urge to wrap her immediately in his arms.

"Hi," he said, instead, feeling breathless.

"Hi," she returned.

He could hear the boys in the kitchen.

"Is everything okay?" he asked.

He searched her expression for a sign of her mood or her state of mind. At first, he'd taken her request as a good sign. But as the minutes dragged by in the jet, he was assailed with doubts. The truth was, he had no idea what she wanted.

"You came," she said.

"Of course I came." Nothing could have kept him away. "Is it the boys?"

"They're fine. We're all fine. Well, maybe not so fine."

Deacon was leaping from hopeful to worried to confused.

"Come in," she said, stepping out of the way.

He walked over the familiar threshold, feeling more at peace and at home than he had in weeks.

"I can't live in the castle," she said.

Hope flooded him. "I would never ask you to live in the castle."

The castle was a terrible place. He had no intention of living there either.

"I know it's a lot of money," she said.

"The money doesn't matter." The money couldn't matter less. "You matter. The boys matter."

"You said you loved me."

"I do."

"What do you love about me?"

"Everything." Without conscious thought, he moved closer to her.

"You haven't talked yourself into it, have you? You know, because of the potential perks of loving me."

He couldn't help but smile at that. "I haven't talked myself into a thing. After you left, if I could have talked myself out of loving you, I would have done it in a heartbeat to save my sanity."

She tilted her head to the side as if she were considering him. "I didn't exactly understand that, but I'm going to assume it was a good thing."

"It was a good thing. It is a good thing." He gave into his desire to reach for her, cradling her face with his palm and stepping closer still. "I love you, Callie, more than anything else in the world."

"You'll give up the money, hundreds of millions of dollars."

"See, the thing is—"

She put her fingertips across his lips. "There can be no equivocation. You have to make your choice."

"There is no equivocation. It's you, Callie, and James and Ethan, over and above anything else in the world."

"Good. Then we'll get by. We have the bakery. We'll work as hard as we have to."

He opened his mouth to explain again, but then thought better of it. "I know we will."

"Good," she repeated.

"So…" He searched her expression. "We're doing this? We're making it real? We're making it work?"

"I love you," she said.

His heart sang, and his grin broke free. "Thank goodness."

He swooped in for a heartfelt kiss.

"Daddy!" came Ethan's excited voice.

"Daddy!" James chimed in.

Ethan's compact body hit the side of Deacon's leg, his little arms going around it. James came up on the other side to give his hip a hug.

Deacon gave Callie another quick kiss. "Hold that thought." Then he crouched down to hug the boys.

"We *are* a package deal," she said with a thread of laughter.

"Best package in the world," Deacon said to the boys.

"Daddy, come and see the new castle," Ethan said, tugging on Deacon's hand.

"It has a moat," James added. "Mommy made us build it in the kitchen."

Deacon looked up at Callie. "Mommy's very smart."

Deacon followed the boys, his boys, to the kitchen, duly admiring their creation.

After a few minutes, he stood, leaning on the counter next to Callie. He took her hand. He touched her cheek. He gave her another kiss.

"There's something you need to know," he said.

She drew back to look at him. “Will I be unhappy?”

“I don’t know. It’s about the money and the Clarksons.”

“That never makes me happy.”

The boys squealed and zoomed rubber alligators through the makeshift moat.

“It’s Aaron and Beau. They want us to be real brothers.”

She searched his expression. “Is that what you want?”

“It is.” It was what Deacon wanted. He was surprised by how much he wanted it.

Callie wrapped her arms around his waist. “Then that’s wonderful.”

Deacon didn’t want to leave anything out. “That’s not the crux of it. They want to join forces with me in running Hale Harbor Port. They blocked Tyrell’s plan to write me out of the company.”

She pulled back again. “The money?”

“It’s still mine. It’s ours. We own Frederick’s share of Hale Harbor Port. And someday it will belong to James and Ethan.” He held his breath, waiting to see if she’d be angry.

She didn’t look thrilled, but she didn’t look angry either.

“You don’t mind?” he dared ask. “That we’re rich and we’re connected to the Clarksons? I promise you don’t have to worry about Tyrell or Margo or anyone else. Any relationship with them will be on your terms.”

“We were always going to be connected to the Clarksons,” Callie said with resignation. “I just didn’t know it for a while.”

“Between me and my brothers—that’s so odd to say. With the three of us together, Tyrell won’t be able to bully anyone ever again.”

James shouted out, “The alligator ate the princess!”

"Owie alligator," Ethan called.

"I'm not afraid of Tyrell," Callie said, molding against him. "I'm through being afraid of bullying men."

"Good."

She gave a little laugh. "I'll send them to you."

"Absolutely."

"You can bribe them."

"Ouch," he said.

"I'm teasing. I have complete faith in you to protect us."

"I always will," Deacon said, feeling a deep and enormous sense of satisfaction. He tightened his hold. "I have a family," he whispered in wonder. "A true and wonderful family. And I love you all so very much."

"We love you back, Deacon. All three of us love you right back."

* * * * *

If you liked this BILLIONAIRES AND BABIES *novel*
from Barbara Dunlop
don't miss her other books in this series!

THE BABY CONTRACT
ONE BABY, TWO SECRETS

Or her WHISKEY BAY BRIDES *trilogy!*

FROM TEMPTATION TO TWINS
TWELVE NIGHTS OF TEMPTATION
HIS TEMPTATION, HER SECRET

Available now from Harlequin Desire!

***

And don't miss the next
BILLIONAIRES AND BABIES *story,*
BILLIONAIRE'S BARGAIN,
by USA TODAY *bestselling author Maureen Child*
Available June 2018!

***

If you're on Twitter, tell us what you think of
Harlequin Desire! #harlequindesire

COMING NEXT MONTH FROM

Available June 5, 2018

#2593 BILLIONAIRE'S BARGAIN

Billionaires and Babies • by Maureen Child

When billionaire Adam Quinn becomes a baby's guardian overnight, he needs help. And his former sister-in-law is the perfect woman to provide it. She's kind, loving and she knows kids. The only complication is the intense attraction he's always tried to deny...

#2594 THE NANNY PROPOSAL

Texas Cattleman's Club: The Impostor • by Joss Wood

Kasey has been Aaron's virtual assistant for eight months—all business and none of the pleasure they once shared. But the salary he offers her to move in and play temporary nanny to his niece is too good to pass up—as long as she can resist temptation....

#2595 HIS HEIR, HER SECRET

Highland Heroes • by Janice Maynard

When a fling with sexy Scotsman Brody Stewart leaves Cate Everett pregnant, he's willing to marry her...*only* for the baby's sake. No messy emotional ties required. But when Cate makes it clear she wants his heart or nothing, this CEO better be prepared to risk it all...

2596 ONE UNFORGETTABLE WEEKEND

Millionaires of Manhattan • by Andrea Laurence

When an accident renders heiress Violet an amnesiac, she forgets about her hookup with Aidan...and almost marries the wrong man! But when the bar owner unexpectedly walks back into her life, she remembers everything—including that he's the father of her child!

#2597 REUNION WITH BENEFITS

The Jameson Heirs • by HelenKay Dimon

A year ago, lies and secrets separated tycoon Spence Jameson from analyst Abby Rowe. Now, thrown together again at work, they can barely keep it civil. Until one night at a party leaves her pregnant and forces Spence to uncover the truths they've both been hiding...

#2598 TANGLED VOWS

Marriage at First Sight • by Yvonne Lindsay

To save her company, Yasmin Carter agrees to an arranged marriage to an unseen groom. The last things she expects is to find her business rival at the altar! But when they discover their personal lives were intertwined long before this, will their unconventional marriage survive?

A year ago, lies and secrets separated tycoon Spence Jameson from analyst Abby Rowe. Now, thrown together again at work, they can barely keep it civil. Until one night at a party leaves her pregnant and forces Spence to uncover the truths they've both been hiding...

Read on for a sneak peek at REUNION WITH BENEFITS by HelenKay Dimon, part of her ***JAMESON HEIRS*** *series!*

Spencer Jameson wasn't accustomed to being ignored.

He'd been back in Washington, DC, for three weeks. The plan was to buzz into town for just enough time to help out his oldest brother, Derrick, and then leave again.

That was what Spence did. He moved on. Too many days back in the office meant he might run into his father. But dear old Dad was not the problem this trip. No, Spence had a different target in mind today.

Abigail Rowe, the woman currently pretending he didn't exist.

He followed the sound of voices, careful not to give away his presence.

A woman stood there—*the* woman. She wore a sleek navy suit with a skirt that stopped just above the knee. She embodied the perfect mix of professionalism and sexiness. The flash of bare long legs brought back memories. He could see her only from behind right now but that angle looked really good to him.

Just as he remembered.

Her brown hair reached past her shoulders and ended in a gentle curl. Where it used to be darker, it now had light brown highlights. Strands shifted over her shoulder as she bent down to show the man standing next to her—almost on top of her—something in a file.

Not that the other man was paying attention to whatever she said. His gaze traveled over her. Spence couldn't exactly blame him, but nothing about that look was professional or appropriate. The lack of respect was not okay. As far as Spence was concerned, the other man was begging for a punch in the face.

As if he sensed his behavior was under a microscope, the man glanced up and turned. His eyebrows rose and he hesitated for a second before hitting Spence with a big flashy smile. "Good afternoon."

At the intrusion, Abby spun around. Her expression switched from surprised to flat-mouthed anger in the span of two seconds. "Spencer."

It was not exactly a loving welcome, but for a second he couldn't breathe. The air stammered in his lungs. Seeing her now hit him like a body blow. He had to fight off the urge to rub a hand over his stomach. Now, months later, the attraction still lingered…which ticked him off.

Her ultimate betrayal hadn't killed his interest in her, no matter how much he wanted it to.

If she was happy to see him, she sure hid it well. Frustration pounded off her and filled the room. She clearly wanted to be in control of the conversation and them seeing each other again. Unfortunately for her, so did he. And that started now.

8308